Edward H. Mathews

PAPER PILOT

Paper planes that actually fly

PENGUIN BOOKS

To Corlia and George

Wynand, many thanks for the excellent work

PENGUIN BOOKS

Published by the Penguin Group
Penguin Books Ltd, 27 Wrights Lane, London W8 5TZ, England
Penguin Books USA Inc., 375 Hudson Street, New York, New York 10014, USA
Penguin Books Australia Ltd, Ringwood, Victoria, Australia
Penguin Books Canada Ltd, 10 Alcorn Avenue, Toronto, Ontario, Canada M4V 3B2
Penguin Books (NZ) Ltd, 182-190 Wairau Road, Auckland 10, New Zealand

Penguin Books Ltd, Registered Offices: Harmondsworth, Middlesex, England

First published in South Africa by E. H. Mathews, Faerie Glen, 1990
Published in Penguin Books 1991
10 9 8 7 6 5 4 3 2 1

Text and plans by E. H. Mathews and C. Mathews
Original figures and layout by C. Mathews, N. W. van der Walt and E. H. Mathews
Photographs by H. J. Visser

Printed in Hong Kong by Imago Publishing Ltd

ABOUT THE AUTHOR

Edward Mathews, who was born in the small country town of Lichtenburg, South Africa, in 1957, has been fascinated by aircraft since his youth. He became an aeronautical engineer and private pilot and currently holds a Ph.D in mechanical engineering and a professorship at the University of Pretoria in South Africa. He has written and published three books on paper planes.

Professor Mathews is very active in research and has received various local and international awards for his work on heat and fluid flow. He has published more than forty papers in journals and conference proceedings and is the guest editor of one international journal and a member of the editorial board of another. His research group has developed software that is in use in twenty-seven countries; their latest aeronautical research project is a high-performance hang-glider.

CONTENTS

1. INTRODUCTION

The paper planes given in this book fly far better than one would imagine. For example, an experienced paper pilot can, under favourable conditions and with a new launching technique discussed in this book, obtain **flight distances of over 100 metres** with some of the models! The fact that there are many similarities between flying paper planes and flying full-scale aircraft, makes the idea of constructing and flying the paper planes even more exciting. It will be shown in this book that the paper pilot has to trim the planes in a manner similar to that used by a pilot of a full-scale aircraft.

An award winning paper pilot should know something about the theory of flight. This will therefore be discussed in Chapter 2. The pilot will also need a well-constructed plane and must further be experienced in launching and trimming the planes. Chapter 3 gives general construction hints which are applicable to all models. (Detailed instructions for constructing the individual planes are given in Chapter 5.) Chapter 4 deals with flight instructions, which not only include conventional launching techniques, but also **a new revolutionary** one. Detail on trimming the planes is also given.

With your background acquired in Chapters 2 to 5 on the theory of flight, paper plane construction and trimming for good flight, the next logical step would be to design your own paper planes and helicopters. This is dealt with in Chapters 6 and 7.

ALWAYS BE VERY CAREFUL NOT TO HIT OTHER PEOPLE WITH YOUR PLANES AND DO NOT FLY THEM NEAR ROADS !

2. THEORY OF FLIGHT

How does a well designed plane stay airborne? Firstly its wings produce enough lift and secondly it is designed and trimmed in such a manner that all the forces acting on it are balanced.

How is lift produced by a plane's wing? In the figure below we see a cross-section of a wing moving through the air. The lines around the wing give an indication of the air-flow. These lines are sometimes called streamlines. Air can only flow from left to right between the streamlines. No flow can cross these lines.

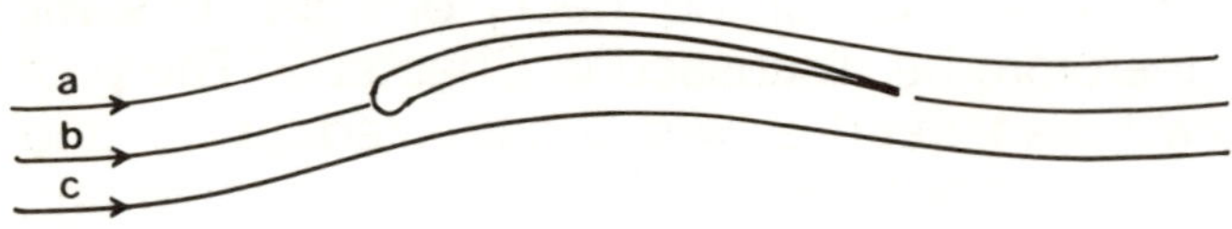

The streamlines are spaced evenly in front of the wing. However, the spacing of these lines differ above and below the wing. These spacings also differ from that in front of the wing. Air-flow over the top of the wing must accelerate to pass through the smaller gap between the top streamlines.

The sum of the velocity and pressure energy between streamlines a and b must be the same in front and on top of the wing. This means that for a higher air velocity on top of the wing, the pressure has to decrease there. In the same manner we can reason that the pressure underneath the wing must increase. The difference in pressure between the upper and lower part of the wing gives rise to an upward force which is called the lift. It is this lifting force that keeps an aircraft airborne.

Now that we have sorted out how the wing produces lift, we can proceed to investigate the other important forces acting on a plane. Remember that a paper plane can only fly successfully if all these forces are balanced. The forces are shown in the figure below. The drag force (D) results from the wind resistance of the plane, while the weight force (W) depends on the mass of the plane. The tail lift (T) is necessary to ensure stable flight. The magnitude of the tail lift can be changed by bending (trimming) the horizontal tail fin (elevator) up or down. This will cause the plane to climb or dive.

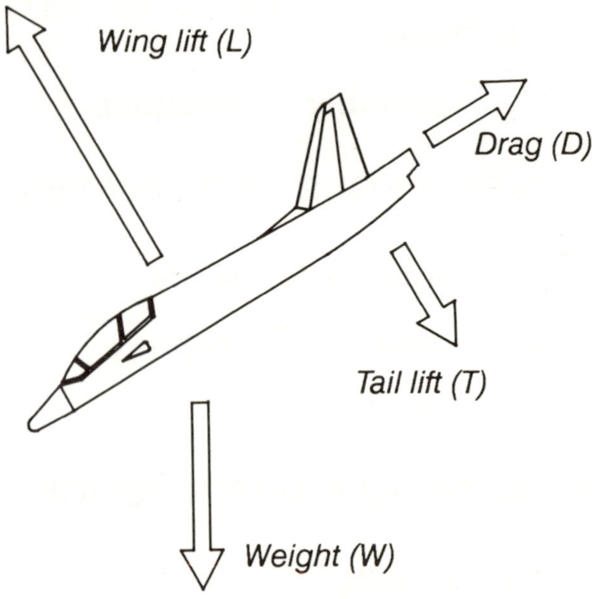

The distance a paper plane can travel also depends on the forces acting on the plane. The next figure shows the relationship between the different forces and the distance (d) a paper plane can travel after being released at height (h).

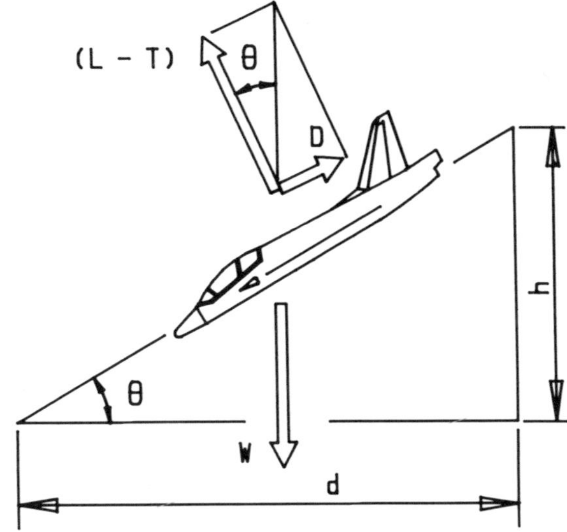

It is clear that, given height (h), a maximum distance (d) can be attained if the glide angle (θ) is kept as small as possible. This can be achieved by ensuring that the following ratio is as large as possible (see the figure above) :

$$d / h = (L - T) / D \qquad (1)$$

This ratio is often referred to as the lift-to-drag ratio of the plane. One of the easiest ways to increase this value for a paper plane is to decrease the drag (D) on its wings. The next figure shows that a curved or cambered wing offers less resistance to the wind than one that is not cambered.

Typical lift-to-drag ratios at cruising flight, for very high performance gliders, are in the order of 50. Equation (1) now shows that for every metre above ground level, the high performance glider can travel 50 metres before touching the ground. This ratio for some of the paper planes in this book, namely the CESSNA Caravan, FAMA PAMPA, SIAI MARCHETTI, SEAPLANE, ROCKWELL B-1B and GRUMMAN HAWKEYE is approximately 8, that is if the planes are well assembled and correctly trimmed. This means that when these planes are launched 8 metres into the air they can travel a distance of roughly 65 metres in windless conditions. **With the help of a slight breeze, flight distances of up to 80 metres have been achieved with these planes** when using conventional launching techniques ! The average flight distances are usually between 40 and 50 metres.

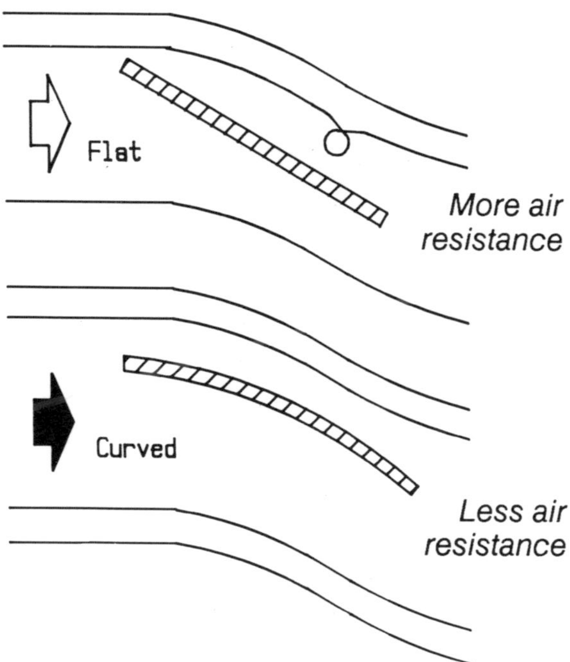

For spectacular and long distance flights, the paper pilot must be able to trim the planes to ensure that all the forces on the plane are balanced in such a way that the plane does not dive, climb or roll excessively. In Chapter 4 the trimming of your planes will be discussed in detail. However, a few general remarks at this stage should be helpful. The elevator or horizontal tail is used to generate forces which prevent excessive climbing or diving (pitching motion), while the vertical fin or stabilizer is trimmed to ensure forces for directional stability (yaw).

Elevator generates necessary vertical forces (Pitching motion)

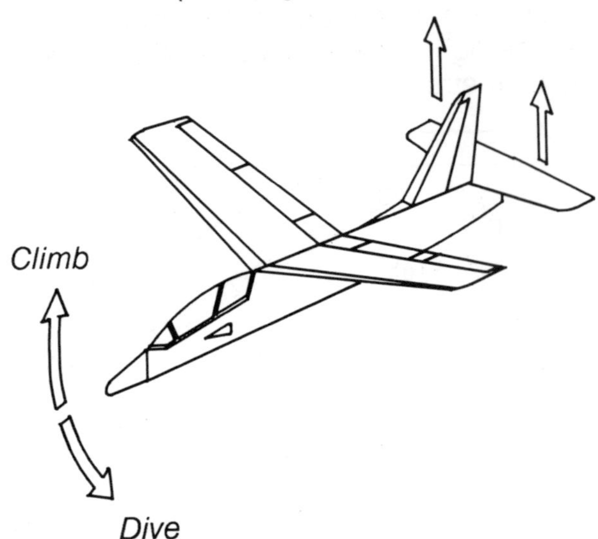

Nose goes left or right (Yawing motion)

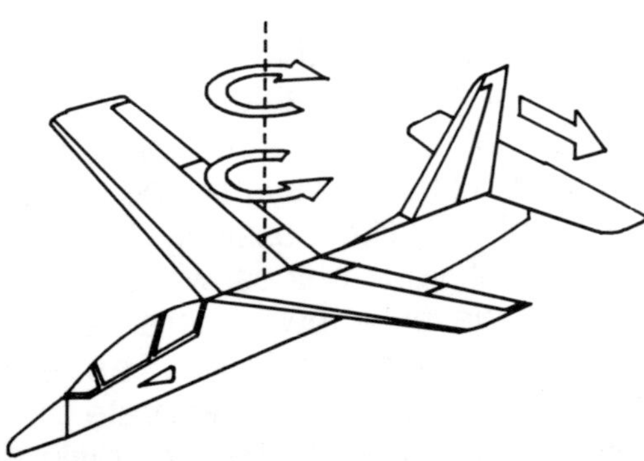

Vertical stabilizer ensures necessary side forces

The wings must be trimmed to prevent the plane from rolling. It must always be symmetrical when viewed from the front to ensure that the forces are balanced on both wings.

Symmetric wing ensures balanced wing forces

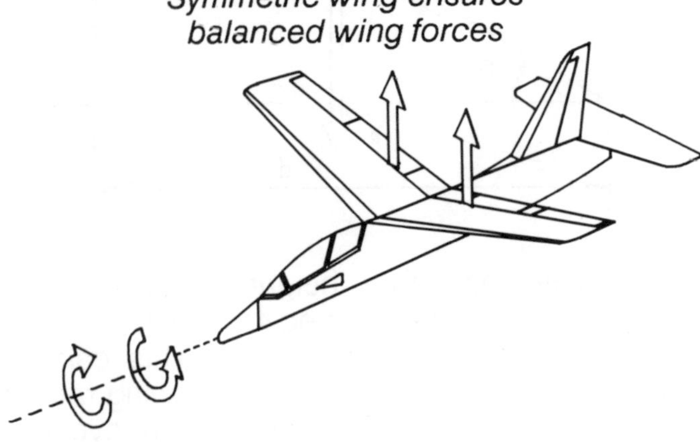

Rolling if forces are not balanced

In summary the following :

- We have discussed how lift is generated by a wing in order to keep a paper pilot's planes aloft.
- It was also shown that a paper plane's lift-to-drag ratio must be as large as possible to enable long distance flights. This can be attained by curving or cambering the wings.
- To ensure long distance flights the paper pilot must further trim the planes to the extent that all the forces are balanced.

3. CONSTRUCTION TIPS

3.1 In this chapter some general construction tips are given. Detailed assembly instructions for the different planes are given in Chapter 5.

3.2 The following tools and materials are needed:

- a pair of sharp scissors,
- cold or white or PVA or wood glue (e.g. Henkel Ponal),
- ruler,
- Prestik or Plasticine,
- paper clips,
- pliers,
- rubber bands,
- a pin,
- good quality cotton thread (e.g. Zwicky).

3.3 Firstly, cut out all the parts on the plans.

3.4 Bend the tabs, which are on some parts, along the dotted lines shown on the plans. Use a ruler to make a neat fold.

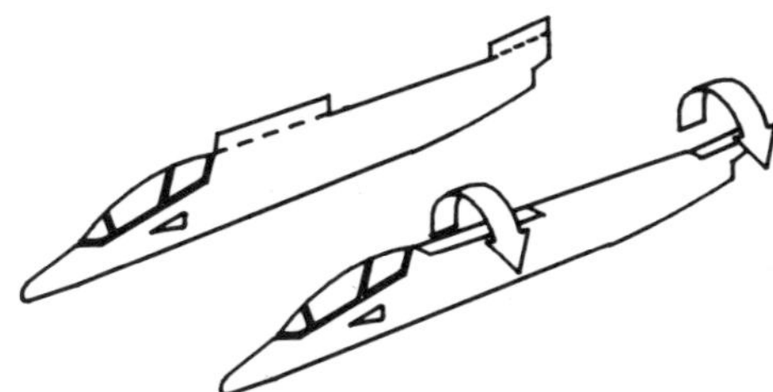

Bend tabs

3.5 The glue must be spread evenly on the parts to be assembled. Use sufficient glue to ensure good construction. Too much glue, however, is not desirable.

3.6 IMPORTANT. Before glueing the wing to the fuselage the wing saddle must be smoothed flat with a ruler.

Flatten the wing attachment saddle with a ruler

Wing saddle

Cross section through fuselage

3.7 There must be no gap between the fuselage and the wing. Ensure that the wing is securely glued to the fuselage.

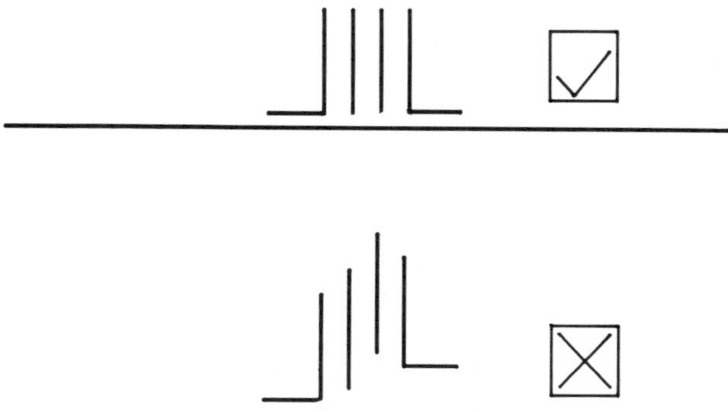

Cross section through fuselage (View from the front)

3.8 After the glue has dried, the plane can be finished. (Henkel Ponal glue takes $\pm$ 20 minutes to dry.)

3.9 Bend the wings upwards to the required dihedral angle. Use the template provided to ensure that the angle is correct.

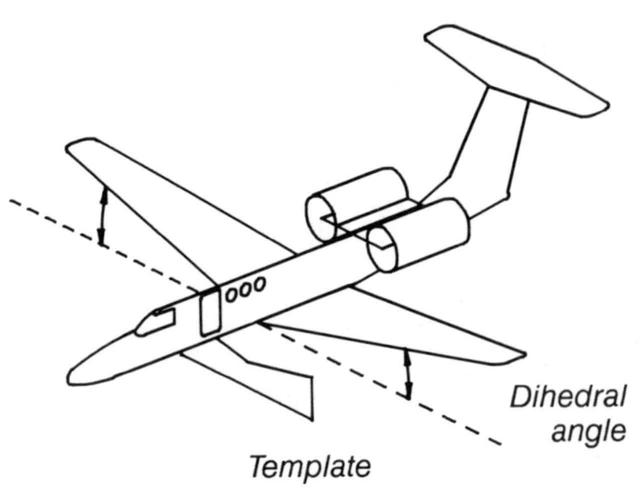

Low wing

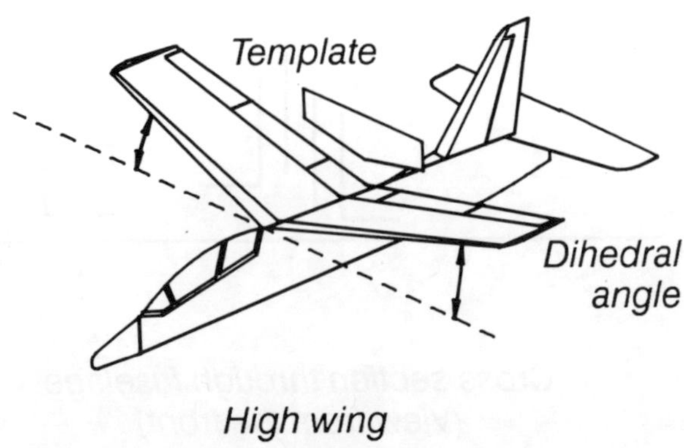

High wing

3.10 For high performance flights the wings must be curved or cambered. The camber profiles are given on the plans.

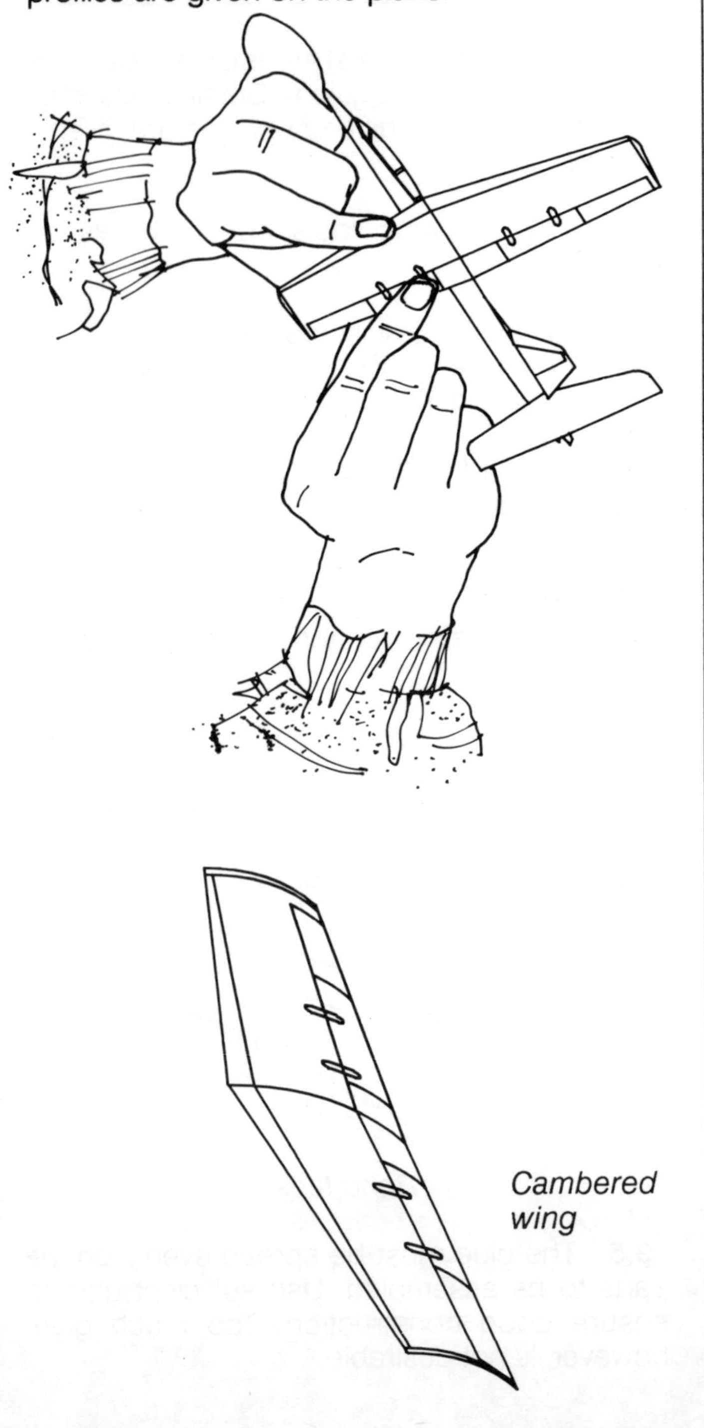

3.11 The plane's centre of gravity must be located at the A mark. By adding Prestik or Plasticine to the nose, the plane can be balanced around the A mark. Use a pair of scissors or tweezers to balance the plane around the A mark.

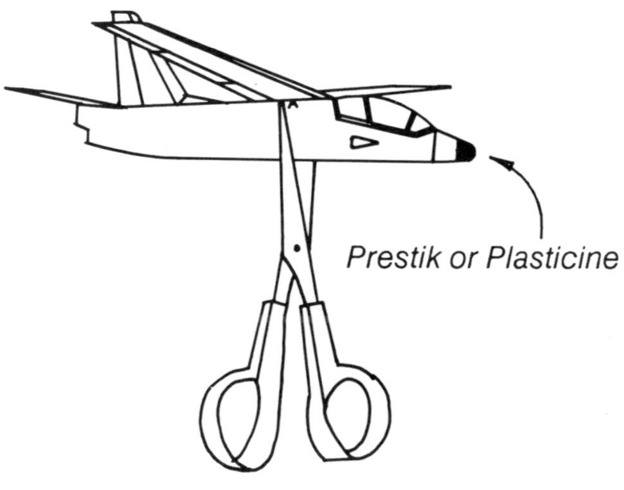

High wing

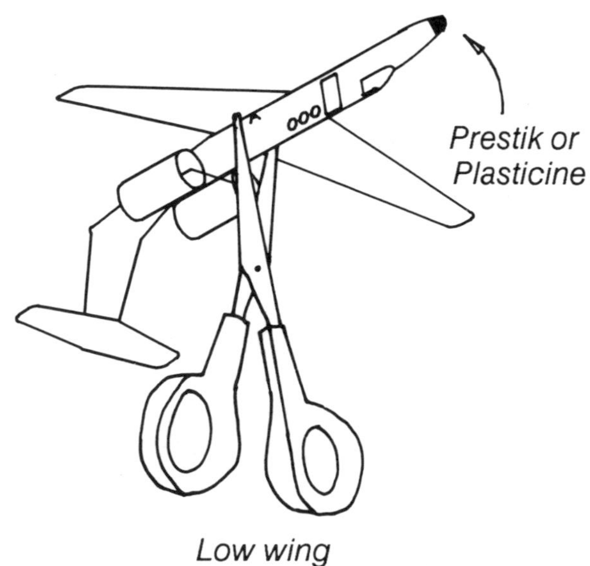

Low wing

3.12 Make a rubber band catapult to launch some of the planes. For best performance the total length of the rubber band must be at least 15 cm.

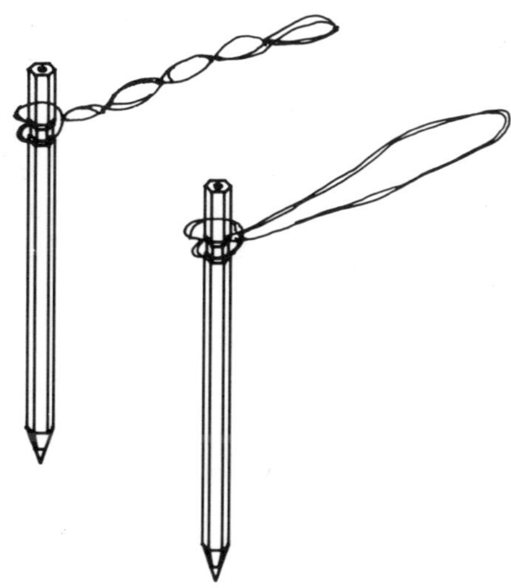

3.13 If the planes get damaged, use glue and pieces of left-over cardboard to fix them.

3.14 If there is movement between the wing and fuselage due to not following the guidelines in paragraphs 3.6 and 3.7 or due to damage, fasten the wing to the fuselage with a piece of cardboard.

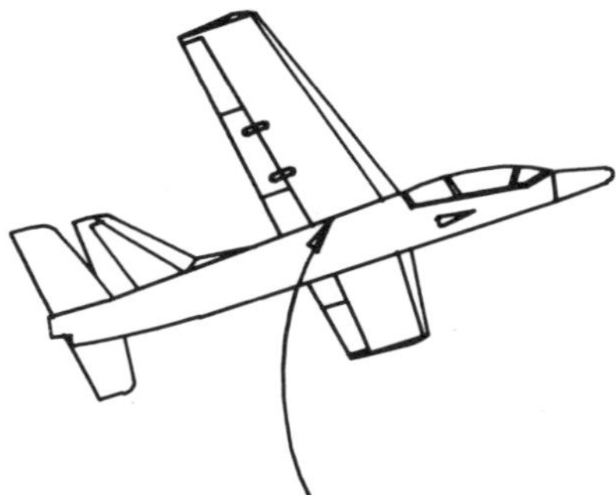

Reinforce with piece of cardboard

4. FLIGHT INSTRUCTIONS

4.1 Check the plane to see if all the parts have bonded well. If not, glue the relevant parts together.

4.2 A paper plane can only fly successfully if it is not warped. (The plane will for example be warped if it was sat on.) Straighten out any warps, bends and twists before you go flying.

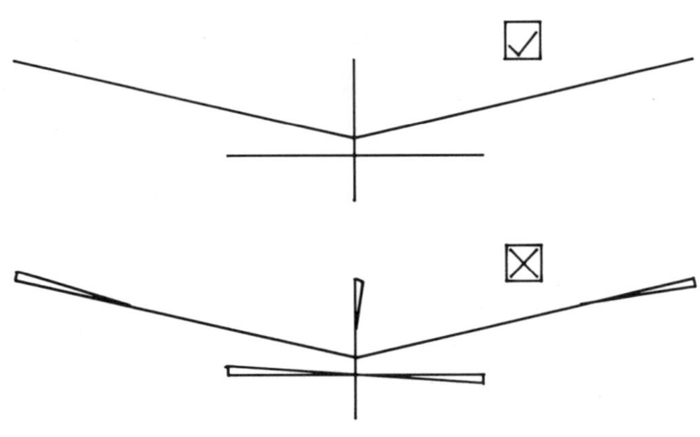

4.3 Any aircraft must be subjected to test flights before it can be commissioned. It is also necessary to test fly the paper planes if you want to make successful flights.

4.4 Gently throw or launch the plane into the wind with a rubber band . Do not launch the plane upwards during test flights.

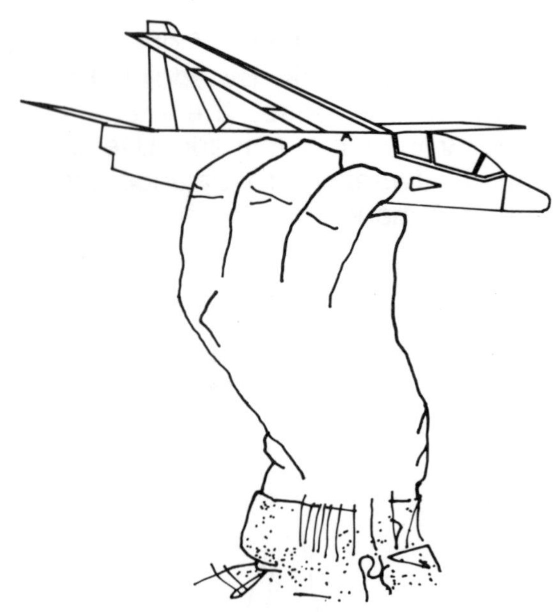

4.5 The plane must fly smoothly in a straight line. If not, make sure that the plane is not bent or warped. (See paragraph 4.2.) If the plane still does not fly in a straight line, it must be trimmed as discussed hereafter.

4.6 IMPORTANT : The paper planes must be well trimmed before flying them. The best trim position of the elevator of a conventional plane, for example, may differ for the same plane of different paper pilots, as the planes are usually not assembled in exactly the same manner by the different pilots. The best trim may also vary according to wind conditions.

Conventional wing

How to trim when the nose goes up. (The reverse applies when the nose goes down.)

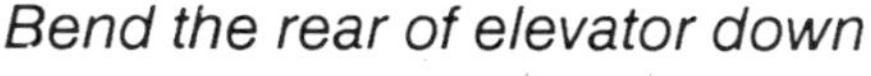

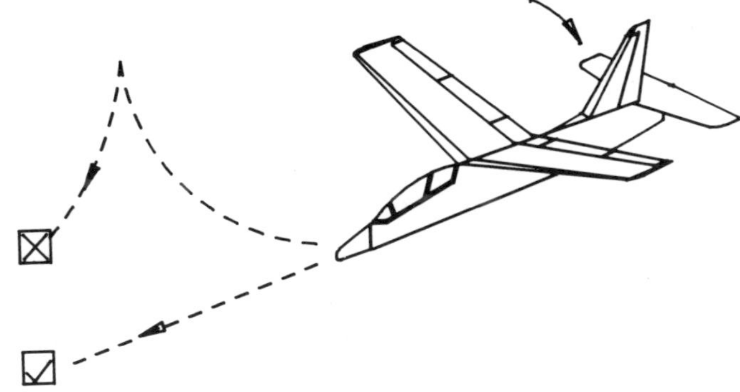

Adjustments needed if the plane curves to the left. (The reverse applies if it turns to the right.)

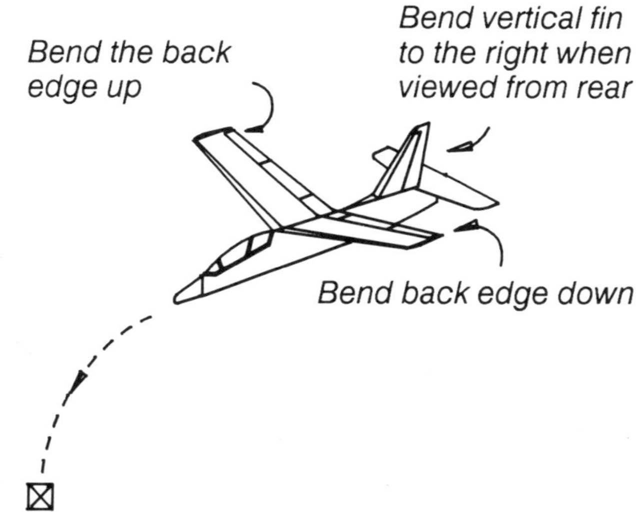

Delta wing

Necessary adjustments when the nose goes up. (The reverse applies when the plane dives.)

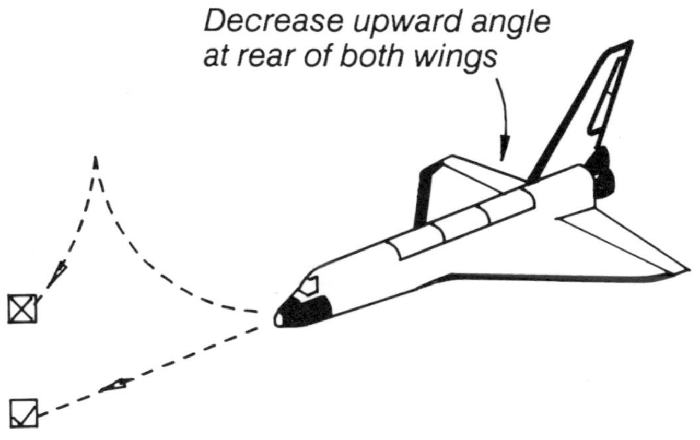

How to trim the plane when it turns to the left. (The reverse applies if the plane curves to the right.)

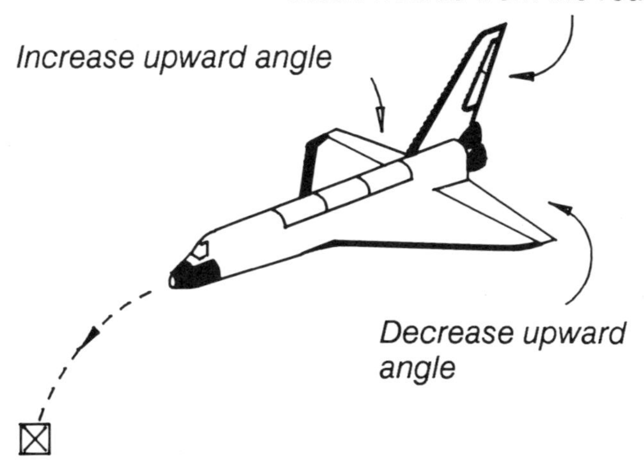

4.7 After successful test flights the plane will be ready for high performance flights.

4.8 If the plane is launched with wings level, into the wind, it will usually make a loop. The plane will thus not make a long flight. To overcome this problem, launch the plane sideways (wings with an angle of 45 degrees to the ground) into the wind.

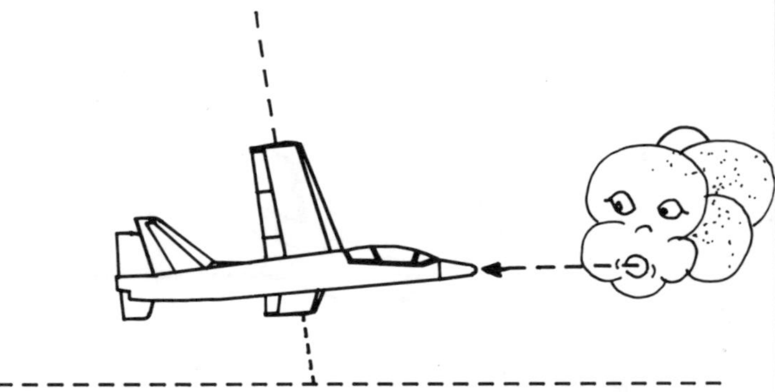

4.9 By launching the plane perpendicular to the wind direction, long flights can often be ensured. The plane can be launched with its wings level or at an angle to the ground.

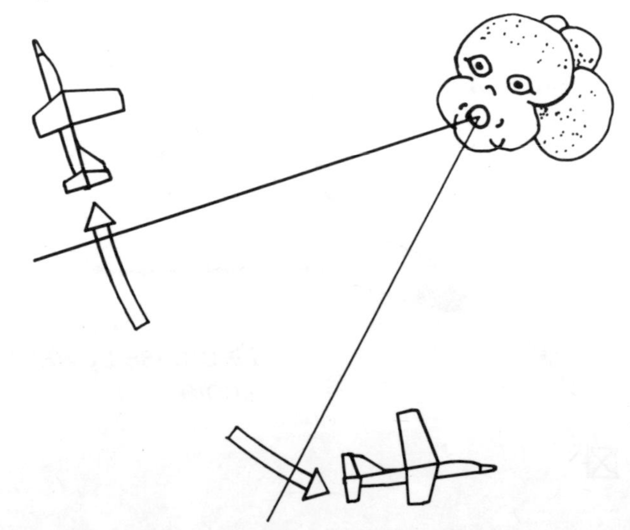

4.10 To attain altitude, the plane can be trimmed to spiral slightly to the left. (See paragraph 4.6.) Launch upwards at a right angle to the direction of the wind. The plane will spiral upwards to the right. At maximum altitude it will spiral downwards to the left.

The reverse of the above procedure can also be used. The plane will then spiral upwards to the left and downwards to the right.

4.11 The planes will fly best when there is a slight breeze. Do not fly planes when the wind is very strong.

4.12 If there is no wind the planes can be launched vertically into the air.

4.13 Just like a real pilot the paper pilot will need some practice to make spectacular flights. It is further suggested to experiment with the above-mentioned launching techniques before using the technique described in the next paragraph.

4.14 By using a **new and revolutionary launching technique** for paper planes, flight distances of **over 100 metres** can be achieved with some of the planes, e.g. the CESSNA Caravan, SIAI Marchetti S.211 and FAMA IA 63 PAMPA. The SHUTTLE can also be launched with this technique.

For the proposed technique very high launching speeds are attained. It is therefore **very important** to ensure that the planes are **well trimmed** before launching them. Also be very careful **not to injure** other people with these high-speed launches. **Ensure that all spectators are always behind you before launching the planes**. As great flight distances can be achieved a large open area, at least the size of one football field, is needed.

Bend an anchoring pin from a piece of wire (e.g. a wire coat-hanger) with approximately the same dimensions as shown in the figure below.

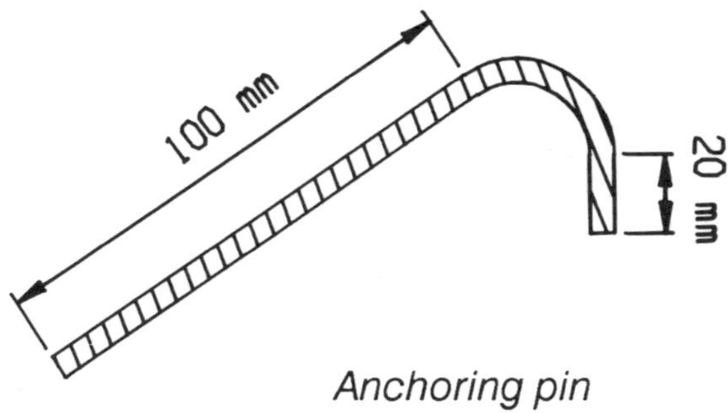

Anchoring pin

Make a bungee to the dimensions shown in the next figure. Use a good quality cotton thread (e.g. Zwicky) and rubber bands. Tie a paper clip to the free end of the cotton thread. Fasten a piece of tissue or toilet paper at a distance of 500 mm from the paper clip. This will help with the release of the paper planes and also help to find the end of the bungee after a launch. Attach the free end of the rubber band to the wire anchoring pin.

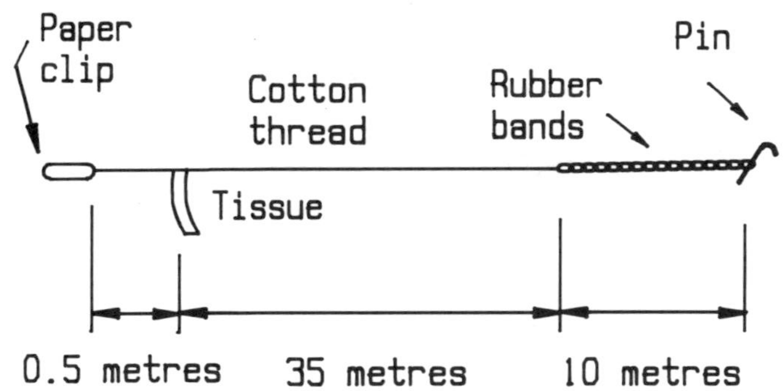

Anchor the bungee to the ground with the wire pin, **upwind** from your launching position (see the figure below). The piece of tissue or toilet paper will indicate the wind direction. Catch the rear hook of the paper plane to the paper clip on the bungee. While holding on to the plane, stretch the bungee a few metres by walking backwards. (As you gain more experience with this technique you can stretch the bungee further.) **Make sure that everybody is behind you**. Tilt the plane at an angle of about 30 degrees and let go !

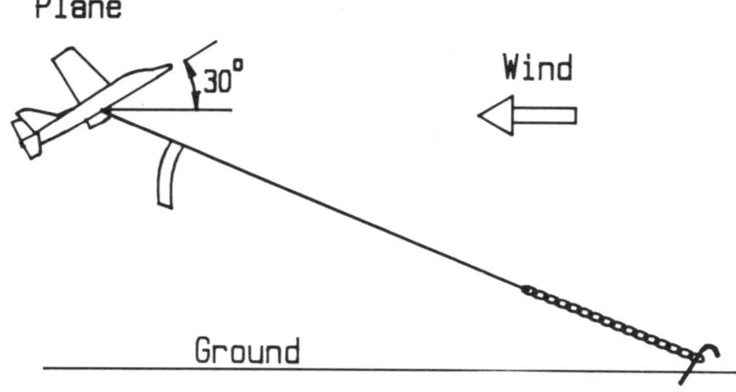

You can experiment with the length to which you stretch the bungee as well as the launch angle of the planes. You can also try to launch the planes as described in paragraph 4.10. Enjoy it !

5. THE PLANES

5.1 TECHNICAL DETAIL

Paper model of SIAI MARCHETTI S.211.

Country of origin : Italy.
Type : Low cost basic trainer and light attack aircraft.
Power plant : One 2 500 lb Pratt & Whitney Canada JT15D-4D turbofan.
Performance : Maximum cruise speed is 667 km/h at 25 000 ft. Maximum service ceiling is 40 000 ft.
Range : A maximum range of 1 668 km can be achieved with 30 minutes reserves.
Weight : Maximum take-off weight is 3 150 kg.
Accommodation : Flight crew of two.
Armament : Maximum armament weight of 600 kg positioned between four wing stations.
Interesting notes : The first of 3 prototypes flew in April 1981. The first production aircraft flew in October 1984. Singapore, Uganda, Haiti and the Philippine Airforce will use the S.211. It will be assembled in Singapore and the Philippine.

GRUMMAN E-2C HAWKEYE

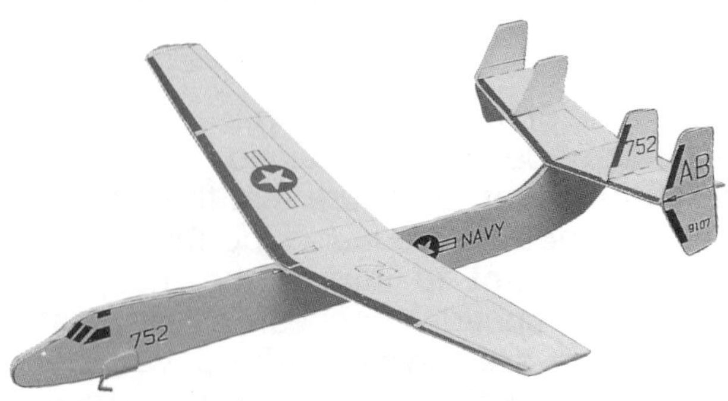

Paper model of GRUMMAN E-2C HAWKEYE.

Country of origin : USA.
Type : Airborne early warning, surface surveillance and strike control aircraft, shipboard or shore-based.
Power plant : Two Allison T56-A-427 turboprops.
Performance : Maximum speed of 598 km/h.
Range : A 3-4 hours ferry range of 2 580 km.
Weight : Maximum take-off weight is 23 556 kg.
Accommodation : Flight crew of five.
Interesting notes : The first E-2C prototype flew in January 1971 and by the beginning of 1989 a 107 have been delivered to the US Navy. Numerous aircraft were also exported to Israel, Japan, Egypt and Singapore. The E-2C evolved from the E-2A and outclasses its predecessor in its capability in target detection and tracking over land.

ROCKWELL B-1 BOMBER

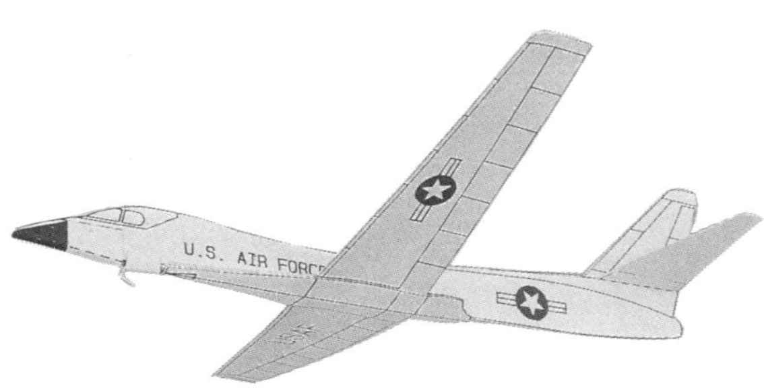

Paper model of ROCKWELL B-1 Bomber with wings in forward swept position.

Country of origin : USA.
Type : Strategic bomber and cruise missile carrier.
Power plant : Four 30 780 pounds thrust General Electric F101-GE-102 turbofans.
Performance : Maximum speed of 1 280 km/h (or Mach 1.25) at 36 000 ft.
Range : The approximated unrefuelled range is 12 070 km.
Weight : The B-1B can take off with a maximum weight of 216 367 kg.
Accommodation : Flight crew of four.
Armament : The B-1B can carry various weapons (up to 14 nuclear bombs) in its three fuselage weapons bays as well as missiles on six external stores stations beneath the fuselage.
Interesting notes : The first production B-1B flew in October 1984 and 100 aircraft were delivered to the USAF in April 1988. During 1987 the B-1B established a series of world records in speed and distance.

CESSNA Caravan

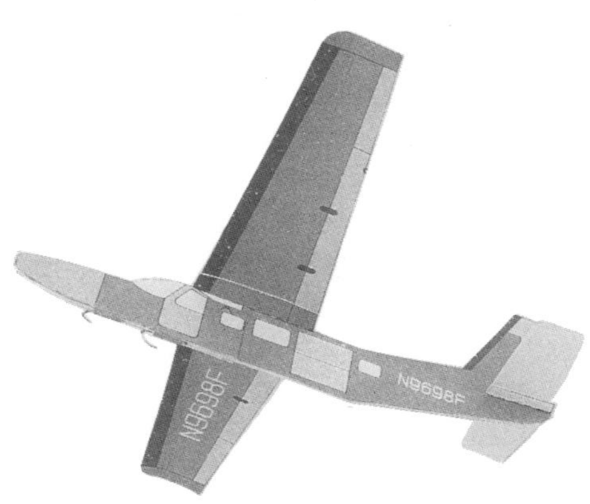

Paper model of CESSNA Caravan.

Country of origin : USA.
Type : Light utility and transport.
Power plant : One 600 shaft horsepower Pratt & Whitney Canada PT6A-114 turboprop.
Performance : Maximum cruise speed at 10 000 ft. of 341 km/h.
Range : 2 010 km (with reserves).
Weight : 3 629 kg (maximum take-off).
Accommodation : Flight crew of two and 14 passengers.
Interesting notes : An engineering prototype was flown for the first time in December 1982. Customer deliveries started in February 1985. By the beginning of 1989 some 300 Caravans had been delivered and the production rate was approximately 8 aircraft monthly. The military uses a derivative, the U-27A, of the Caravan for special missions which include troop transport, medivac, surveillance and forward air control. The U-27A can also be fitted with 6 wing stores stations for gun pods and rockets.

BIZJET model 2C

BIZJET model 2C.

Country of origin : PROPP (Pilot's Republic of Paper Plania).
Type : Light corporate executive transport.
Power plant : Two flow-through Rolls Royce cardboard RR 15D-5A turbojets.
Performance : Maximum cruise speed of 14 km/h at 20 m.
Range : Approximately 60 m depending on weather and experience of pilot.
Weight : Approximately 8 grammes.
Accommodation : Flight crew of one beetle and seven executive insects.
Interesting notes : The latest in the paper plane series of corporate executive transports to attain production, the BIZJET model 2C is expected to surpass earlier aircraft in its class. It differs from its predecessors primarily in having 20 % more power, 8.5 % more speed, 6.25 % more payload and 5 % less empty weight.

SEAPLANE

SEAPLANE.

Country of origin : PROPP (Pilot's Republic of Paper Plania).
Type : Single-engined seaplane. (Please keep away from real water !)
Power plant : One 0.001 shaft horsepower turboprop with freely rotating cardboard prop.
Performance : Maximum cruise speed of 12 km/h at 20m.
Range : Approximately 70 m depending on weather and experience of pilot.
Weight : Approximately 9 grammes.
Accommodation : Flight crew of one beetle and sixteen passengers.
Interesting notes : The first engineering model flew towards the end of 1989 while the first production model flew in April 1990. From the other planes described in this book, it can be seen that for most full-scale aircraft it takes approximately 3 years from the first prototype flight to the first flight of a production model.

FAMA IA 63 PAMPA

Paper model of FAMA IA 63 PAMPA.

Country of origin : Argentina.
Type : Tandem two-seater trainer.
Power plant : One Garrett TFE-371-2-2N turbofan.
Performance : Maximum speed at 7 000 m of 819 km/h.
Range : Maximum range of 1 500 km at 4 000 m at a speed of 556 km/h.
Weight : Maximum take-off weight of 5 000 kg.
Accommodation : Flight crew of two.
Interesting notes : The first prototype flew in October 1984 while the first production model flew in March 1988. The PAMPA was developed by Dornier of Federal Germany on behalf of the Argentine government. This company continues to provide assistance to FAMA in the further development of the PAMPA. A shipboard and various instructional and light attack versions aimed at the export market are foreseen in the near future.

SPACE SHUTTLE

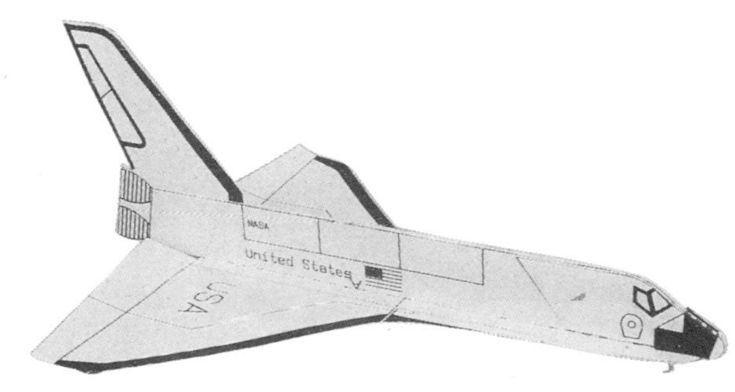

Paper model of SPACE SHUTTLE.

Country of origin : USA.
Type : Re-usable spaceship intended to deliver space payloads into earth orbit.
Power plant : Three main engines delivering 375 000 pounds of thrust each at sea level and 470 000 pounds in space (vacuum). They are assisted for launching purposes by two re-usable solid rocket boosters which generate 2.9 million pounds of thrust at sea level.
Weight : Total weight at lift-off is 1.4 million kg.
Accommodation : A maximum of 10.
Interesting notes : The first SHUTTLE, Enterprise, was put through extensive approach and landing tests in the late seventies. SPACE SHUTTLE Columbia was the first to be launched in April 1981. One aspect that makes the SHUTTLE remarkable is the fact that its flight speeds vary between 20 000 and 200 mph.

BELL 222

Paper model of the BELL 222, the helicopter used for AIRWOLF.

Country of origin : USA.
Type : BELL = Light utility. AIRWOLF = Attack helicopter.
Performance : BELL = 278 km/h. AIRWOLF = Maximum speed above the speed of sound*.
Range : BELL = 691 km. AIRWOLF = Classified information.
Weight : BELL = 3742 kg. AIRWOLF = Information not available.
Accommodation : BELL = Flight crew of one and 9 passengers. AIRWOLF = Flight crew of three.
Interesting notes : The model 222 was the first US light twin-turbine helicopter. The first prototype flew in August 1976. The first production delivery was in 1979.

* *It is interesting to note that the world speed record for real life helicopters is less than half the speed of sound at just over 400 km/h.*

5.2 PLANS

The plans of the paper planes are given in the Appendix. It is preferable to remove the plan pages before cutting out any of the planes' parts.

Part of the fun of paper planes lies in their construction. Furthermore, to ensure good flights, the planes must be well constructed. It is therefore important to follow the assembly instructions carefully.

Remember that for good flights the planes must be well constructed, well trimmed and correctly launched.

NOTE :

Carefully study the assembly instructions in section 5.3 before constructing your planes.

5.3 ASSEMBLY INSTRUCTIONS

SIAI MARCHETTI S.211

A. Glue wing parts (7) and (8) firmly together.

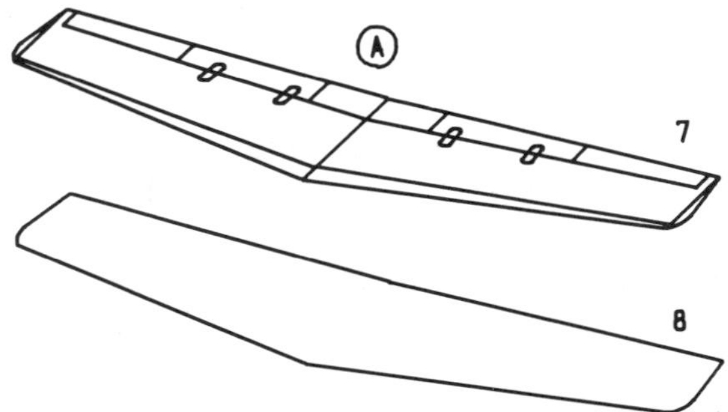

B. Fold all the tabs up along the dotted lines.

C. Paste parts (1) to (6) firmly together.

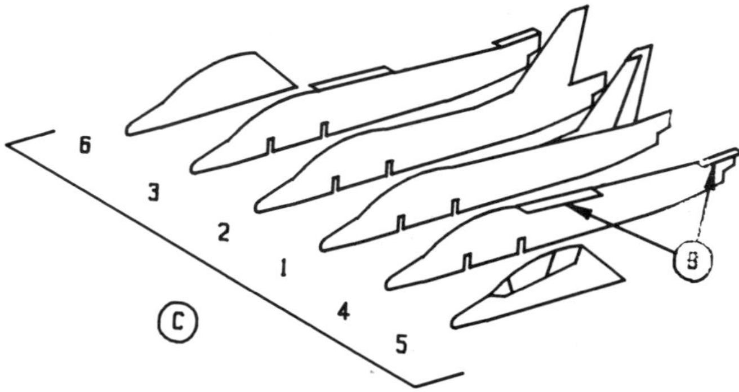

D. Ensure that the wing saddle is correctly prepared. (See paragraph 3.6.) Glue the wing very firmly to the fuselage. (See paragraph 3.7.)

E. Wait for the glue to dry. Paste the elevator (9) to the fuselage. Take the same precautions as for the wing to ensure a firm bond between the elevator and the fuselage.

F. With a pair of pliers bend hooks (10) and (11) from paper clips. **It is very important that the bungee hook (11) must have the exact same dimensions as shown on the plan**. Bond hook (10) and bungee hook (11) firmly to the fuselage with parts (12) and (13).

G. Bend the wing to the desired dihedral angle. Use template (14) to measure if the angle is correct. Glue part (15) onto the wing to ensure that the dihedral angle does not change with time.

H. Shape or camber the wings using part (16) as a template.

I. Put Prestik or Plasticine on the plane's nose to balance the plane around the A mark.

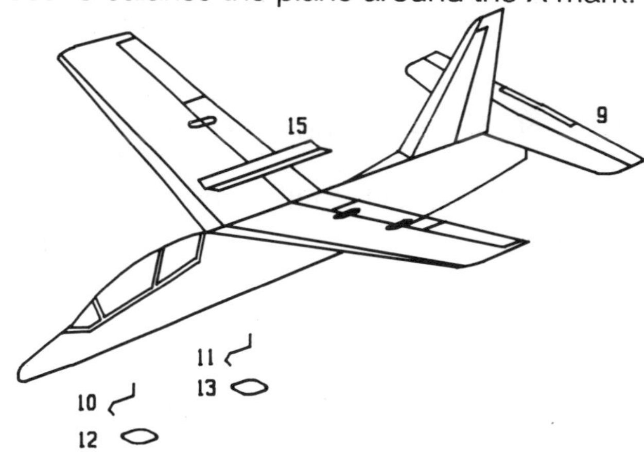

D – I

J. Make sure that the plane is not bent or warped. (See paragraph 4.2.) Do the test flights as prescribed in paragraphs 4.3 to 4.6. After successful test flights and if the plane is correctly launched, the SIAI MARCHETTI can, under favourable weather conditions, **fly up to 80 metres** with the conventional launching techniques and **over 100 metres** with the new technique. *Remember that you must have experience before using the new technique*.

GRUMMAN HAWKEYE

A. Glue wing parts (7) and (8) firmly together. Construct the tail unit by folding the tabs of elevators (9) and (10) up along the dotted lines. Glue these two elevators firmly together. Fold the two tabs of rudders (12) and (13) in different directions. Then glue the four rudders (11), (12), (13) and (14) onto the elevator.

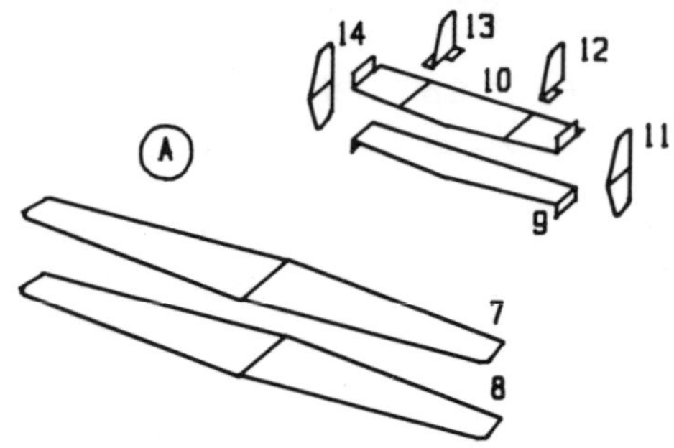

B. Fold all the tabs up along the dotted lines.

C. Paste parts (1) to (6) firmly together.

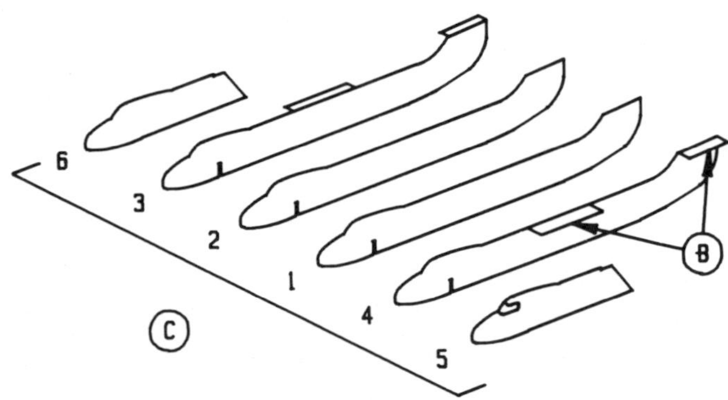

D. Ensure that the wing saddle is correctly prepared. (See paragraph 3.6.) Glue the wing <u>very firmly</u> to the fuselage. (See paragraph 3.7.)

E. Wait for the glue to dry. Paste the tail unit to the fuselage. Take the same precautions as for the wing to ensure a firm bond between the tail unit and the fuselage.

F. Bend hook (15) from a paper clip with a pair of pliers.

G. Bond hook (15) firmly to the fuselage with part (16).

H. Bend the wing and elevator to the desired dihedral angle. Use template (17) to measure if the angle is correct. Glue part (18) onto the wing to ensure that the dihedral angle does not change with time.

I. Curve the wings using part (19) as a template.

J. Put Prestik or Plasticine on the plane's nose to balance the plane around the A mark.

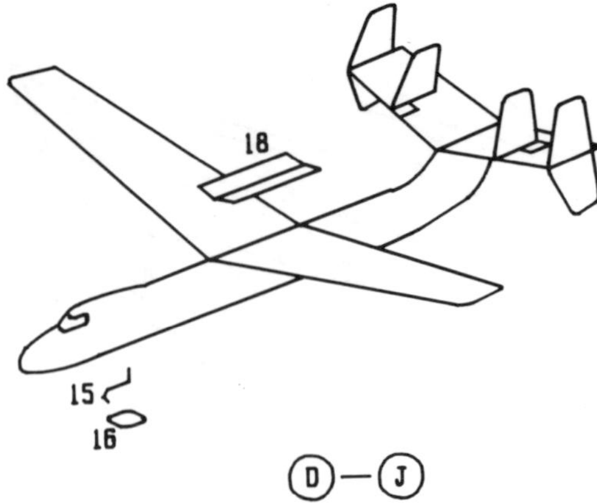

K. Make sure that the plane is not bent or warped. (See paragraph 4.2.)

L. Do the test flights as prescribed in paragraphs 4.3 to 4.6.

M. The GRUMMAN HAWKEYE is stable and flies very well.

ROCKWELL B-1 Bomber

A. Glue wing parts (7) and (8) firmly together.

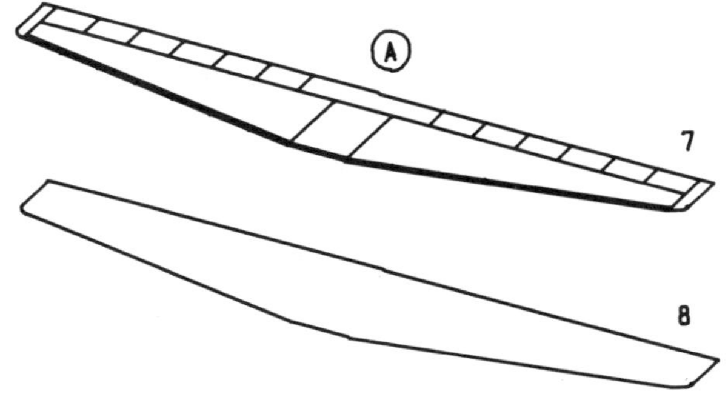

B. Fold all the tabs up along the dotted lines.

C. Paste parts (1) to (6) firmly together.

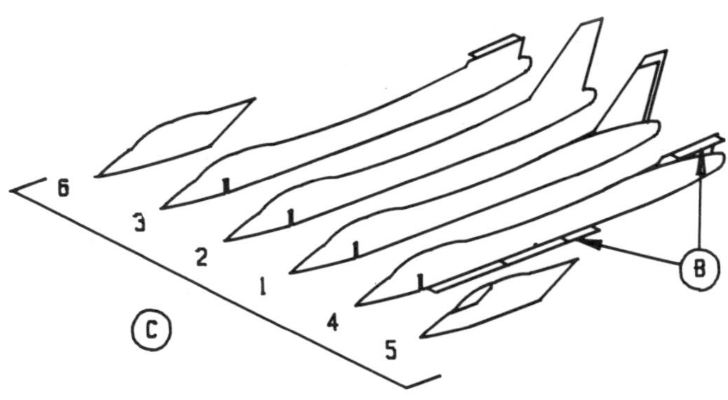

D. Glue part (9) to the nose of the plane.

E. Ensure that the wing saddle is correctly prepared. (See paragraph 3.6). Glue the wing very firmly to the fuselage. (See paragraph 3.7).

F. Glue parts (10) and (11) very firmly to the fuselage. (See paragraph 3.7).

G. Wait for the glue to dry. Paste the elevator (12) to the fuselage. Take the same precautions as for the wing to ensure a firm bond between the elevator and the fuselage.

H. Bend hook (13) from a paper clip with a pair of pliers. Bond hook (13) firmly to the fuselage with part (14).

I. Bend the wing to the desired dihedral angle. Use template (15) to measure if the angle is correct. Glue part (16) onto the wing to ensure that the dihedral angle does not change with time.

J. Shape the wings using part (17) as a template.

K. Put Prestik or Plasticine on the plane's nose to balance the plane around the A mark.

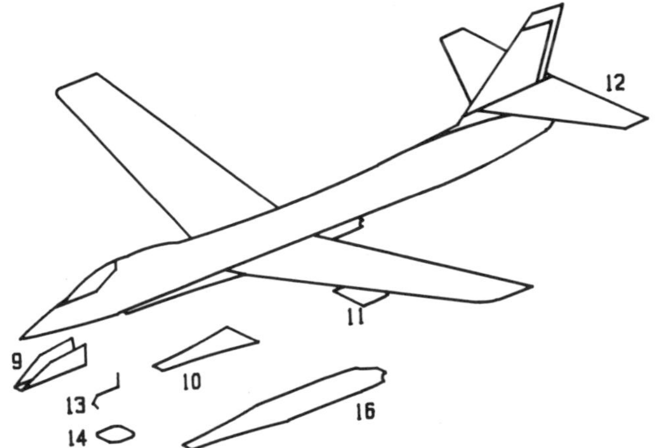

L. Make sure that the plane is not bent or warped. (See paragraph 4.2.) Do the test flights as prescribed in paragraphs 4.3 to 4.6. The B-1 Bomber is a sensitive plane and must be well trimmed. If correctly trimmed, however its flights are spectacular.

CESSNA Caravan

A. Glue wing parts (7) and (8) firmly together.

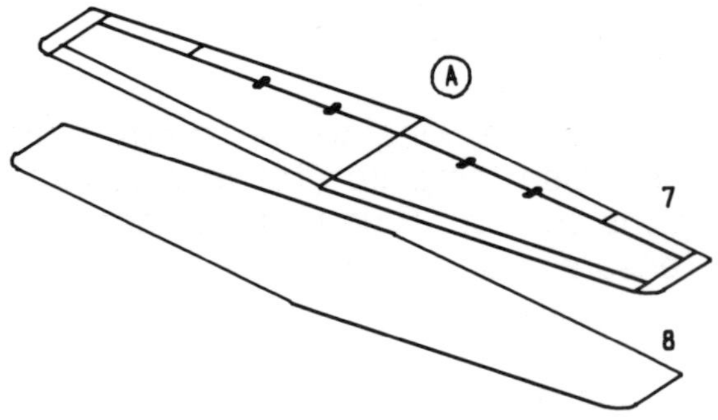

B. Fold all the tabs up along the dotted lines.

C. Paste parts (1) to (6) firmly together.

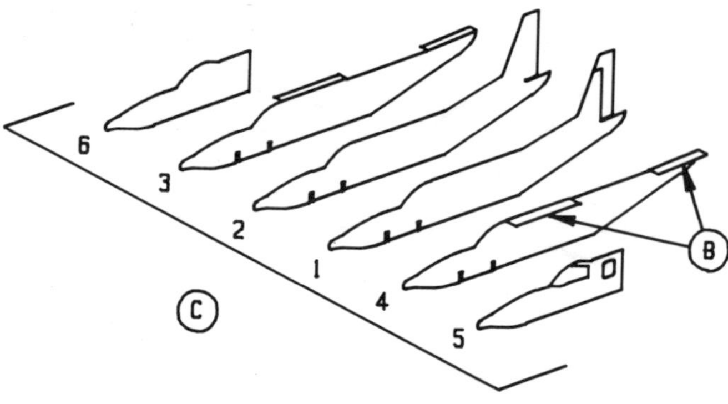

D. Ensure that the wing saddle is correctly prepared. (See paragraph 3.6.) Glue the wing <u>very firmly</u> to the fuselage. (See paragraph 3.7.)

E. Wait for the glue to dry. Paste the elevator (9) to the fuselage. Take the same precautions as for the wing to ensure a firm bond between the elevator and the fuselage.

F. With a pair of pliers bend hooks (10) and (11) from paper clips. **It is very important that the bungee hook (11) must have the exact same dimensions as shown on the plan**. Bond hook (10) and bungee hook (11) firmly to the fuselage with parts (12) and (13).

G. Bend the wing to the desired dihedral angle. Use template (14) to measure if the angle is correct. Glue part (15) onto the wing to ensure that the dihedral angle does not change with time.

H. Curve or camber the wings using part (16) as a template.

I. Put Prestik or Plasticine on the plane's nose to balance the plane around the A mark.

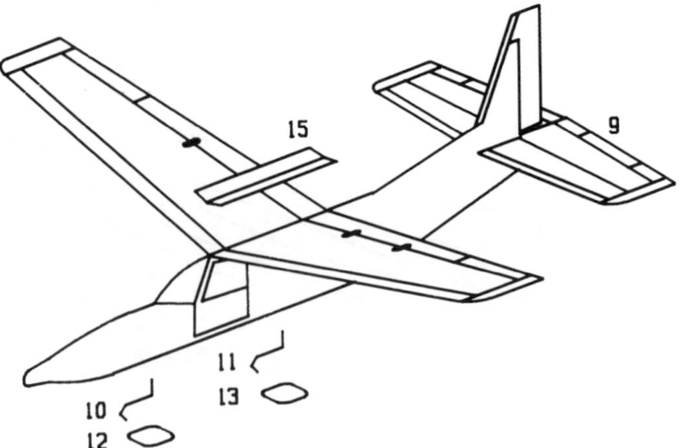

J. Make sure that the plane is not bent or warped. (See paragraph 4.2.) Do the test flights as prescribed in paragraphs 4.3 to 4.6. The CESSNA Caravan flies well if all the instructions are carefully followed. The CESSNA is one of the planes that can be launched with the new launching technique. *You must be fairly experienced before using the new technique*.

BIZJET model 2C

A. Glue wing parts (7) and (8) firmly together.

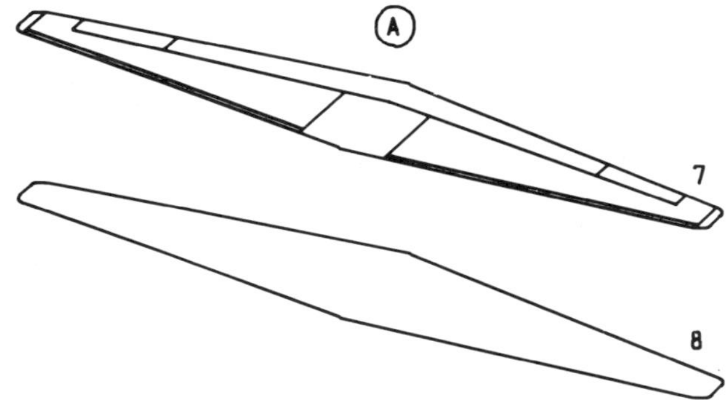

B. Fold all the tabs up along the dotted lines.

C. Paste parts (1) to (6) firmly together.

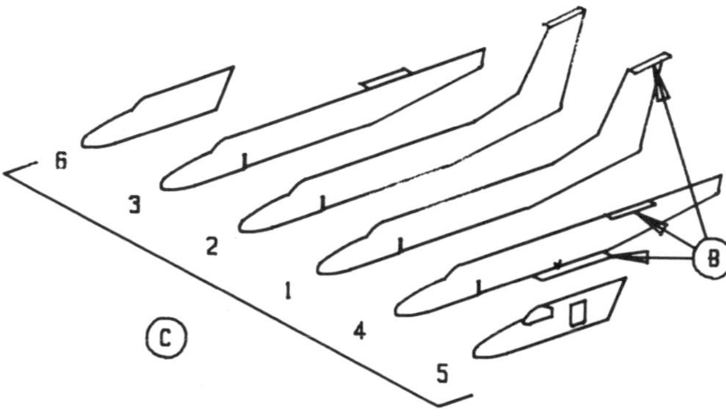

D. Construct the two jet engines by rolling parts (9) and (10) around a pencil. Ensure that they are well bonded where the ends of the paper overlap.

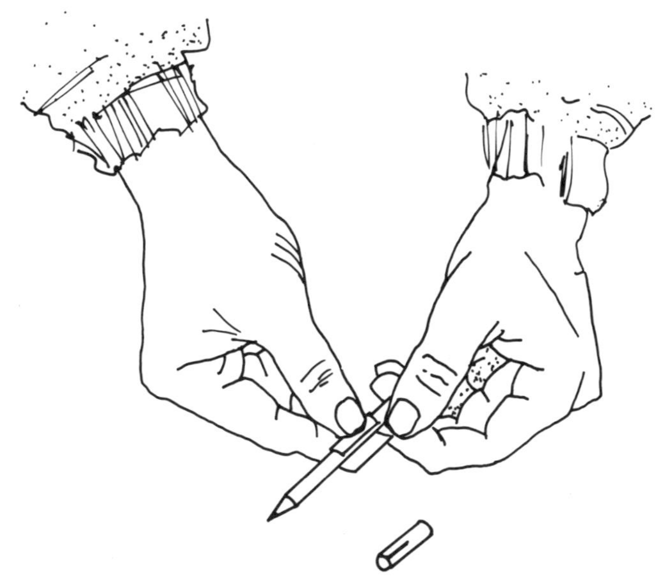

E. Ensure that the wing saddle is correctly prepared. (See paragraph 3.6.) Glue the wing very firmly to the fuselage. (See paragraph 3.7.)

F. Wait for the glue to dry. Paste the elevator (11) and the engine pylon (12) to the fuselage. Take the same precautions as for the wing to ensure a firm bond between these parts and the fuselage. Glue the engines to the pylon (12).

G. Bend hook (13) from a paper clip with a pair of pliers.

H. Bond hook (13) firmly to the fuselage with part (14).

I. Bend the wing to the desired dihedral angle. Use template (15) to measure if the angle is correct. Glue part (16) onto the wing to ensure that the dihedral angle does not change with time.

J. Shape the wings using part (17) as a template.

K. Put Prestik or Plasticine on the plane's nose to balance the plane around the A mark.

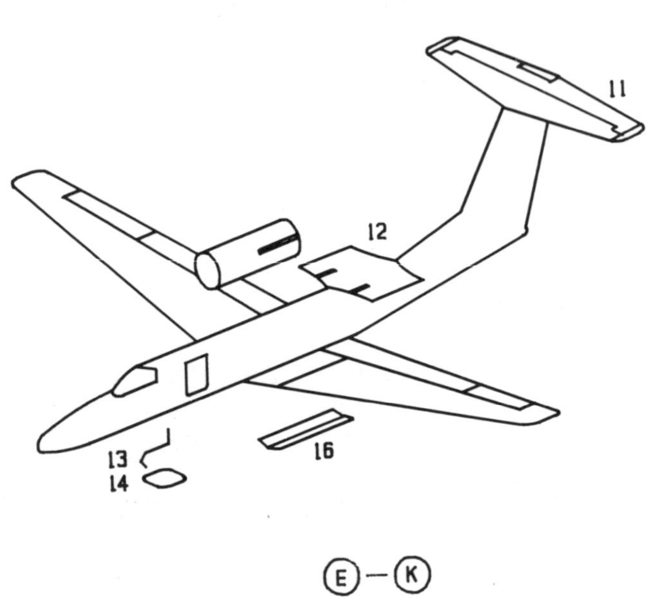

L. Make sure that the plane is not bent or warped. (See paragraph 4.2.)

M. Do the test flights as prescribed in paragraphs 4.3 to 4.6. The BIZJET looks impressive as it jets past you with its two engines. If you want the BIZJET to fly very long distances, remove the two engines to reduce the drag force on the plane.

SEAPLANE

A. Glue wing parts (7) and (8) firmly together.

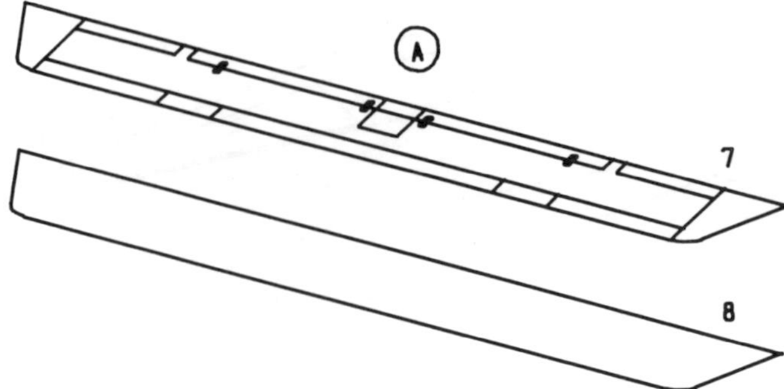

B. Fold all the tabs up along the dotted lines.

C. Paste parts (1) to (6) firmly together.

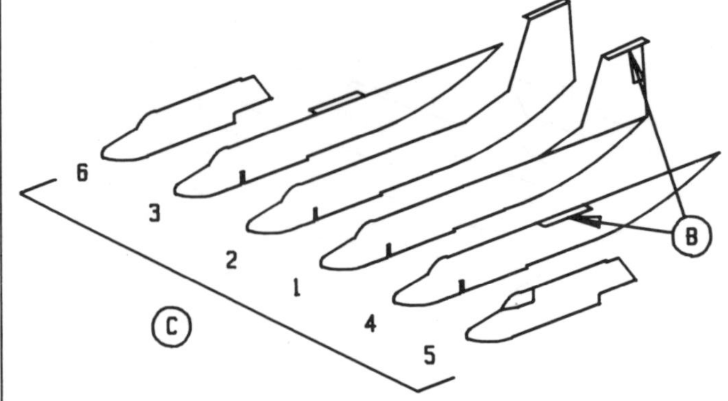

D. Construct the propeller. First make a hub for the propeller by rolling part (9) around a pin. The inside of part (9) must be smeared with glue. The hub should turn easily around the pin. Glue parts (10) and (11) to the hub and to each other. Twist the propeller blades in the opposite directions. If one blade is heavier than the other, cut off small pieces from the heavy blade until it balances nicely around the pin.

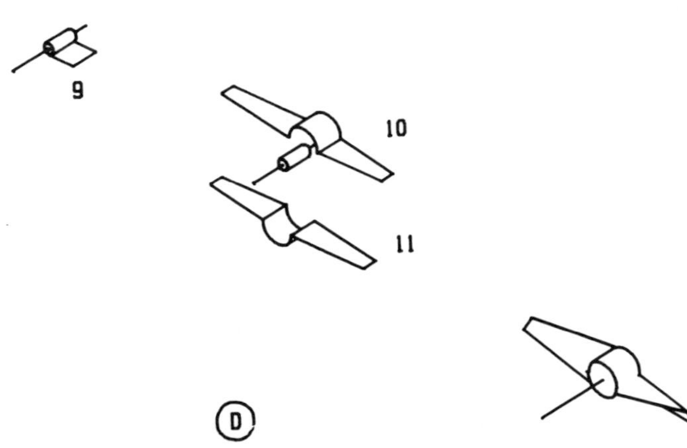

E. Ensure that the wing saddle is correctly prepared. (See paragraph 3.6.) Glue the wing very firmly to the fuselage. (See paragraph 3.7.)

F. Wait for the glue to dry. Paste the elevator (12) to the fuselage. Take the same precautions as for the wing to ensure a firm bond between the elevator and the fuselage.

G. With a pair of pliers bend hook (13) from a paper clip.

H. Bond hook (13) firmly to the fuselage with part (14).

I. Bend the wing to the desired dihedral angle. Use template (15) to measure if the angle is correct. Glue part (16) onto the wing to ensure that the dihedral angle does not change with time.

J. Construct the engine. Glue parts (17) and (18) together. Fold the tabs of parts (19) and (20) up along the dotted lines. Glue parts (17) to (20) firmly together. Glue the engine onto the wing. Insert the pin with the propeller into the engine.

K. Curve the wings using part (21) as a template.

L. Put Prestik or Plasticine on the plane's nose to balance the plane around the A mark.

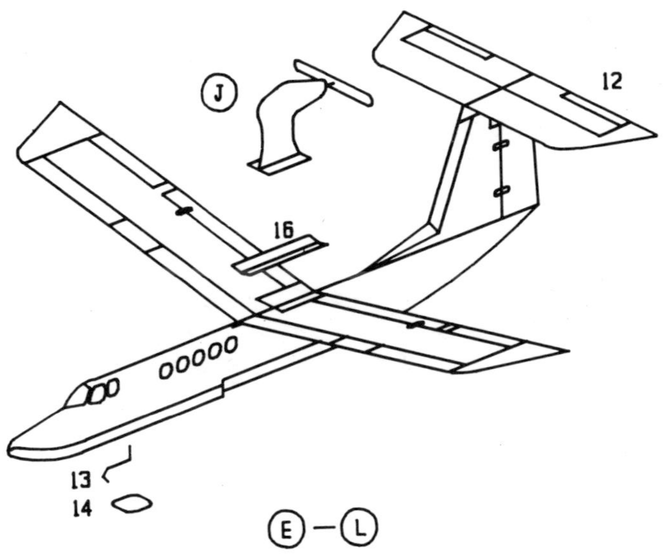

M. Make sure that the plane is not bent or warped. (See paragraph 4.2.)

N. Do the test flights as prescribed in paragraphs 4.3 to 4.6.

O. The SEAPLANE can fly long distances. Listen to the sound of the propeller as it flies past you.

FAMA IA 63 PAMPA

A. Glue wing parts (7) and (8) firmly together.

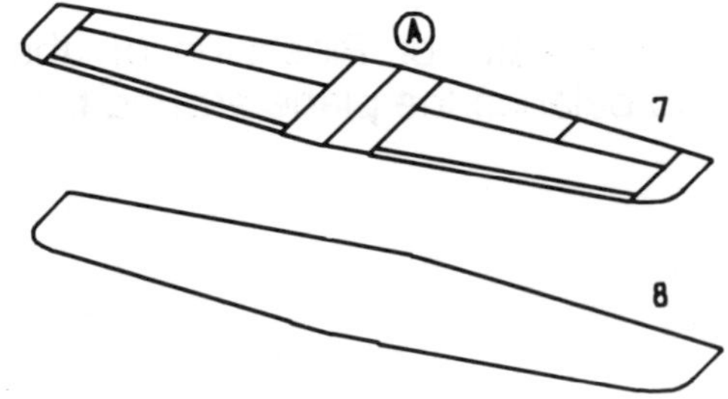

B. Fold all the tabs up along the dotted lines.

C. Paste parts (1) to (6) firmly together.

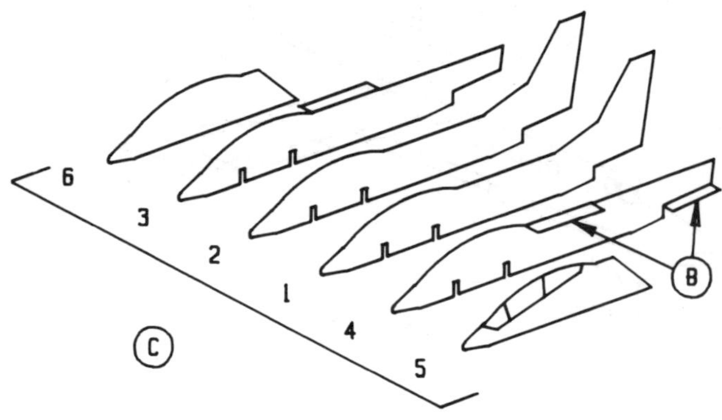

D. Ensure that the wing saddle is correctly prepared. (See paragraph 3.6.) Glue the wing very firmly to the fuselage. (See paragraph 3.7.)

E. Wait for the glue to dry. Paste the elevator (9) to the fuselage. Take the same precautions as for the wing to ensure a firm bond between the elevator and the fuselage.

F. With a pair of pliers bend hooks (10) and (11) from paper clips. **It is very important that the bungee hook (11) must have the exact same dimensions as shown on the plan**. Bond hook (10) and bungee hook (11) firmly to the fuselage with parts (12) and (13).

G. Bend the wing to the desired dihedral angle. Use template (14) to measure if the angle is correct. Glue part (15) onto the wing to ensure that the dihedral angle does not change with time.

H. Shape or camber the wings using part (16) as a template.

I. Put Prestik or Plasticine on the plane's nose to balance the plane around the A mark.

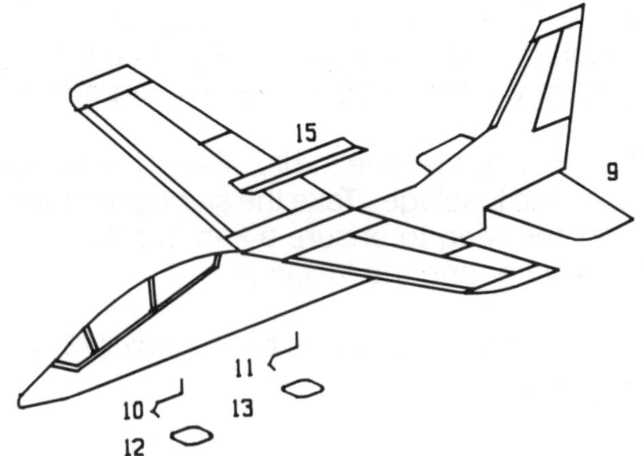

D – I

J. Make sure that the plane is not bent or warped. Do the test flights as prescribed in paragraphs 4.3 to 4.6. The FAMA PAMPA can **fly up to 80 metres** in favourable conditions with the conventional launching techniques and **over 100 metres** with the new technique. *Remember that you must have experience before using the new technique*.

SPACE SHUTTLE

A. Cut out the small holes in wing parts (7) and (8). Glue these parts firmly together.

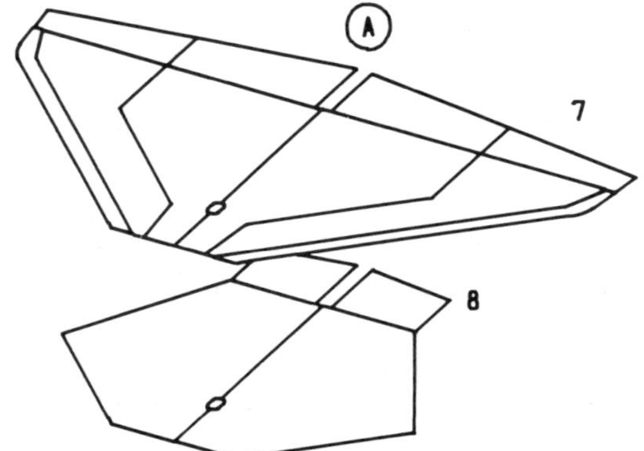

B. Fold all the tabs up along the dotted lines.

C. Paste parts (1) to (6) firmly together.

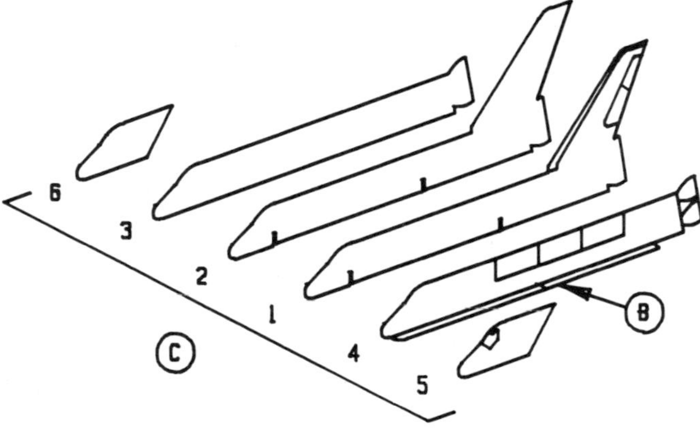

D. Ensure that the wing saddle is correctly prepared. (See paragraph 3.6.) Glue the wing very firmly to the fuselage. (See paragraph 3.7.)

E. Glue part (9) to the fuselage and part (10) to the wing assembly.

F. Glue part (11) to the nose of the plane.

G. With a pair of pliers bend hooks (12) and (13) from paper clips. **It is very important that the bungee hook (13) must have the exact same dimensions as shown on the plan**. Bond hook (12) and bungee hook (13) firmly to the fuselage with parts (14) and (15).

H. Bend the rear of the wing slightly upwards (approximately 2 - 3 mm). Make the bend on the line shown on the wing.

I. Put Prestik or Plasticine on the plane's nose to balance the plane around the A mark.

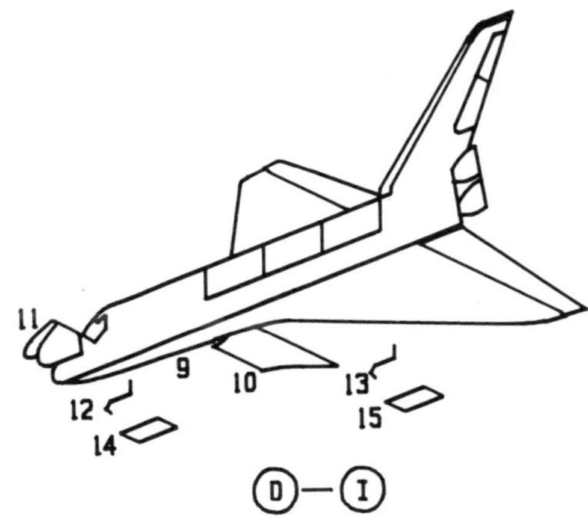

J. Make sure that the plane is not bent or warped. (See paragraph 4.2.)

K. Do the test flights as prescribed in paragraphs 4.3 to 4.6. Launch the plane gently with a rubber band catapult during test flights.The new launching technique (paragraph 4.14) as well as the technique described in paragraph 4.10 works very well for the SHUTTLE. *You must be fairly experienced before using the new technique*. Make sure that the plane does not spiral excessively. It performs very well if correctly trimmed. Notice the true to life approach as the SHUTTLE comes in to land. The SHUTTLE is a fun plane, rather than a high performance glider.

BELL 222, the helicopter used for AIRWOLF

The BELL 222 is more difficult to construct than the other planes in this book. It is advisable to delay its construction until you have gained more experience with the other models.

A. Cut out part (1). Use a compass or a pair of scissors to score the circle marked (A). Bend the part slightly along this scoring mark. See the cross-section in the figure below. Glue ends B' and C' to B'' and C'' respectively. Ensure that ring (1) is not warped.

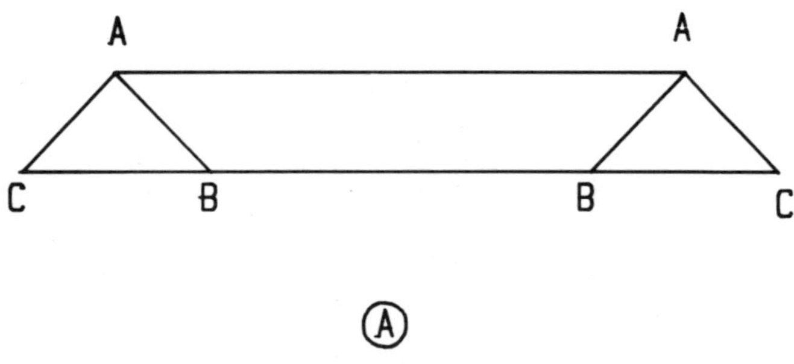

Ⓐ

B. Cut out part (2). Glue the inside (B) and outside (C) of ring (1) to ring (2). Ensure that the indicated arrows overlap.

C. Fold the small outer tabs on ring (2) up along the dotted line (C). It helps to score the dotted folding line (C) with a compass or a pair of scissors before folding these tabs. (DO NOT SCORE THE FOLDING LINES (B) OF THE TRIM TABS.) Glue three tabs on one side of ring (2) onto ring (1). Then do the same with three tabs on the opposite side of the ring. Rotate the ring 90 degrees clockwise and glue another six tabs, three on each side. Now rotate the ring 45 degrees clockwise and repeat the glueing process. Once again rotate the ring through 90 degrees and glue three tabs on opposite sides to ring (1). Glue the rest of the tabs on ring (2) onto ring (1). The trim tabs must not be folded yet.

D. Glue the cross (3) onto the top of ring (2). Then glue strips (4) and (5) to the underside of this ring.

E. Bend a paper clip in the form of shape (6).

F. Construct the rotor. First make a hub for the rotor by rolling part (7) around paper clip (6). The inside of part (7) must be smeared with glue. The hub should turn easily around the paper clip. Glue parts (8) and (9) to the hub and to each other. Twist the rotor blades in the opposite directions. Ensure that the final rotor has a flat bottom as illustrated in the figure.

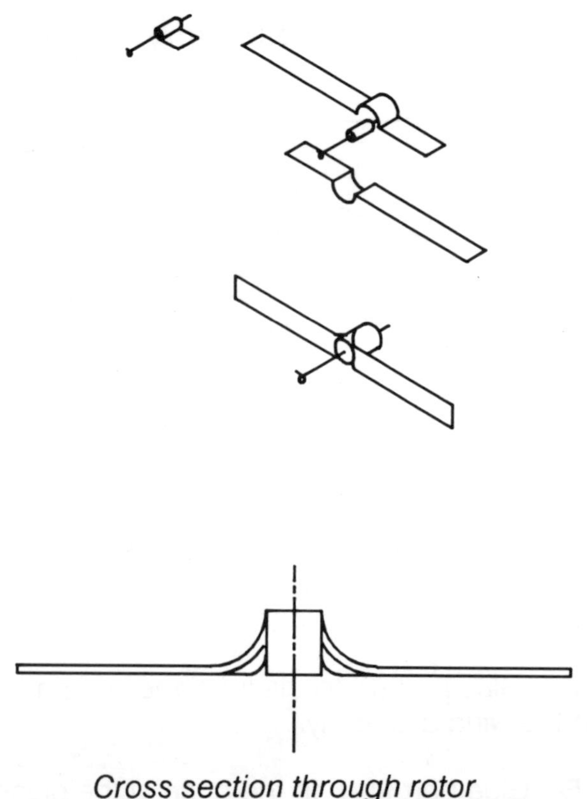

Cross section through rotor

G. Paste the rotor to the bottom of the ring sub-assembly.

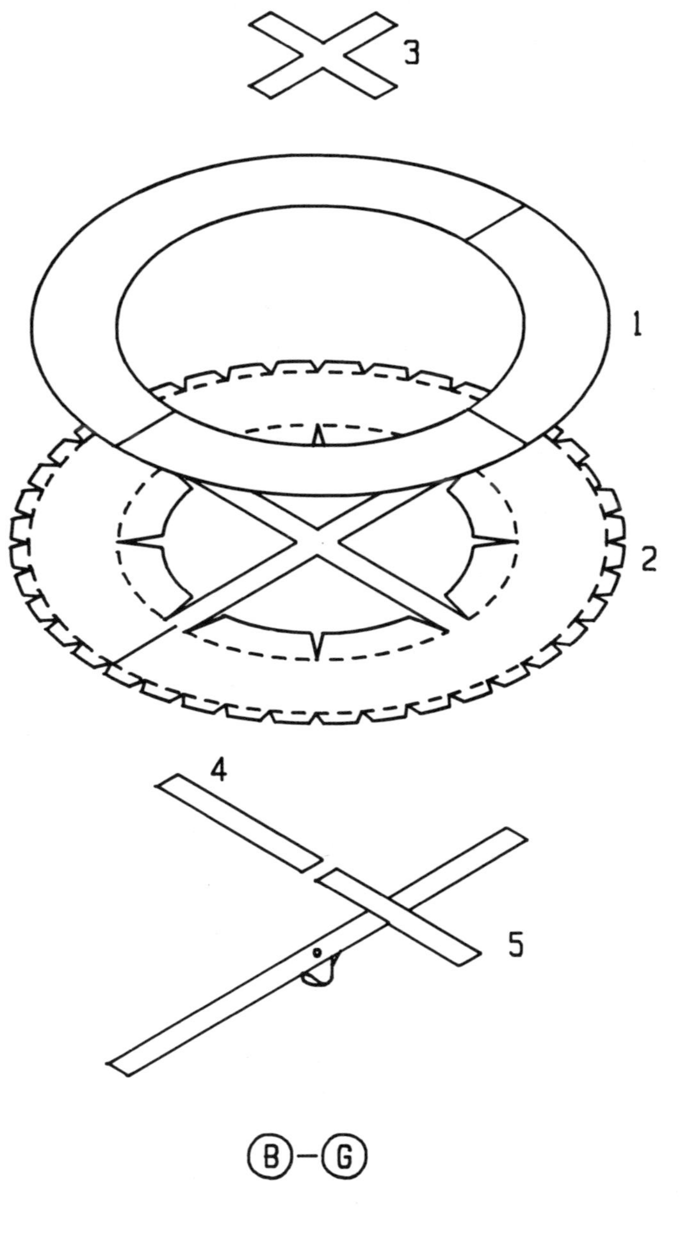

H. Fold all the tabs of parts (10) to (14) up along the dotted lines. Construct the fuselage by glueing parts (10) to (12) firmly together, but do not yet glue part (13). Glue the boom (14) to the folded tabs of the fuselage. Glue fins (15) and (16) onto the boom.

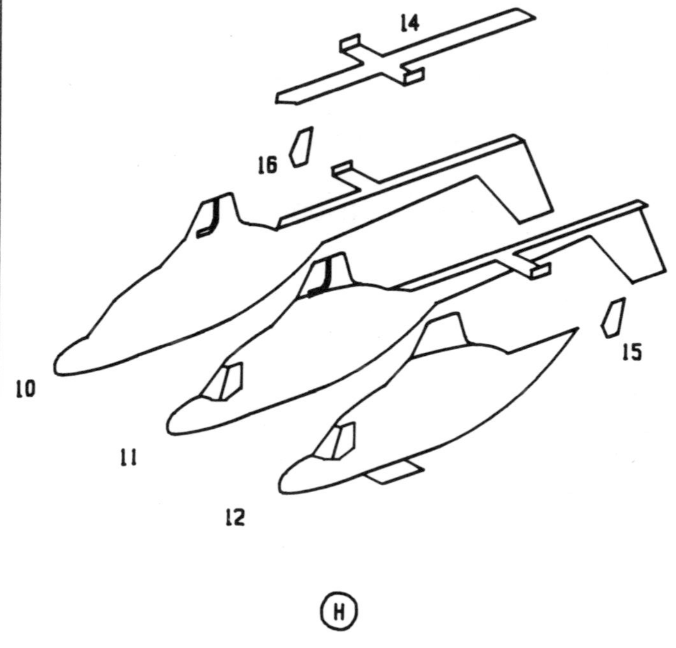

I. Make a hole in the middle of the ring, at the cross, through which the paper clip (6) can slide. Put the paper clip (6) through this hole from the top, right through the ring sub-assembly, including the hub. Ensure that the ring rotates freely around the clip. With the paper clip still in the ring, bend the lower part of the clip to fit into the groove in the fuselage.

J. Place the ring upside down onto a flat surface with the bent paper clip protruding upwards. Now complete the BELL 222 by securing the paper clip to the fuselage. This is done by glueing part (13) firmly over the paper clip onto the fuselage. Glue the gun pod, part (17) onto the fuselage.

K. The BELL 222 flies similar to a frisbee. Take the ring in your right hand and with a wrist spin, throw it gently forwards. As helicopters usually fly slower and have shorter ranges than planes, do not force the BELL 222 to fly too fast or too far. You can expect flight distances of approximately 10 metres with the BELL 222. It further flies exceptionally well in light wind conditions, making it an ideal indoor flyer.

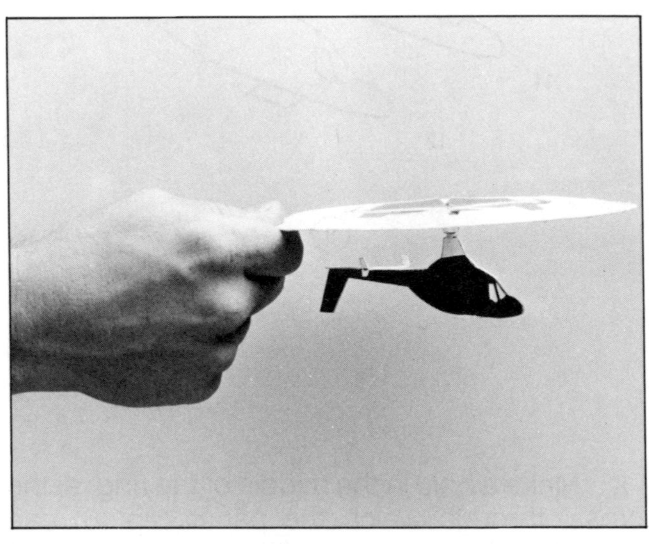

L. Using the trim tabs to control the direction of flight, the BELL 222 will make spectacular flights. If it turns excessively to the left, bend all the trim tabs upwards. If it turns right, bend the tabs down. The opposite procedure must be followed if the BELL 222 is launched with your left hand. Note that its fuselage always turns into the flight direction - true to life !

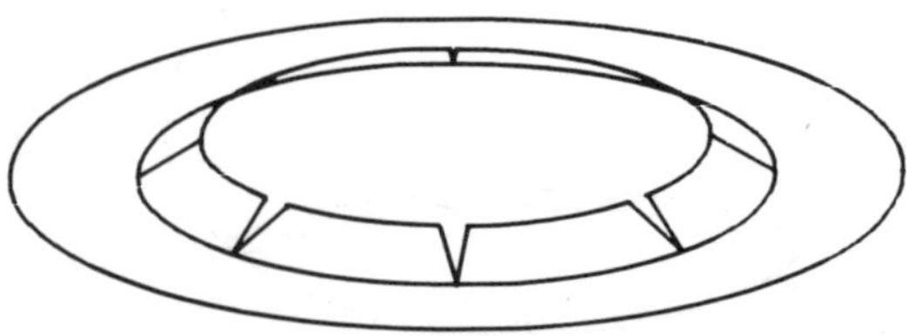

If the BELL 222 turns left fold all the trim tabs upwards

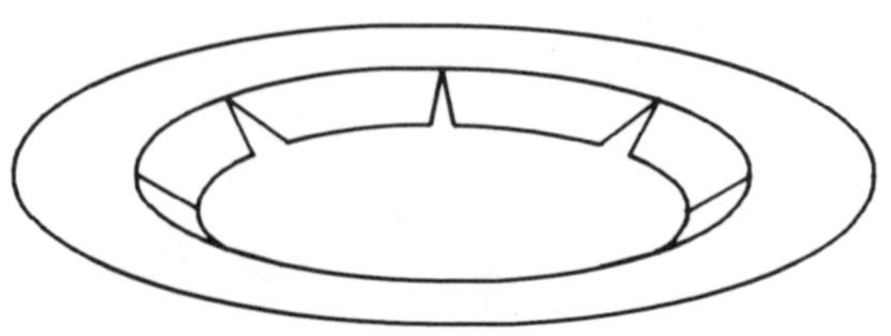

If the BELL 222 turns right fold all the trim tabs downwards

6. DESIGN YOUR OWN PLANES

The most important aspects to consider when designing paper planes, are the following :

- flight performance,
- structural strength,
- stability.

6.1 FLIGHT PERFORMANCE

Good flight performance for paper planes means that they should stay airborne for a reasonable distance. As discussed in Chapter 2 this can be achieved by maximizing the lift-to-drag ratio. One of the easiest ways to increase this value is to decrease the drag on the plane's wings. This is usually done by curving or cambering the wings as shown in paragraph 3.10.

6.2 STRUCTURAL STRENGTH

The paper plane must not deform as a result of the forces acting on it. Structural strength can be achieved by using various layers of paper and ensuring that the direction of stiffness is in the lengthwise direction of the fuselage, wings, and horizontal tail plane.

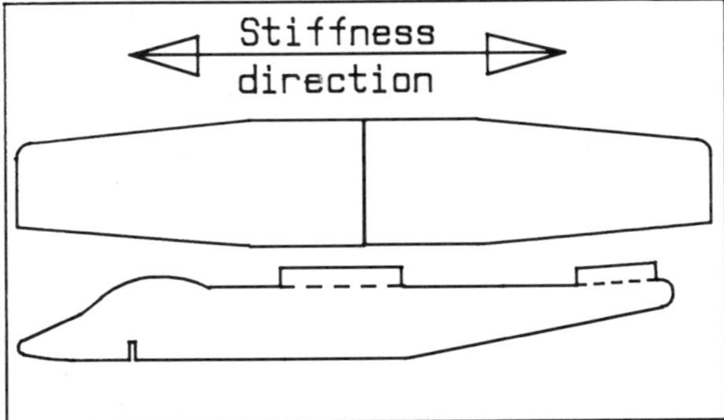

6.3 STABILITY

A paper plane must be stable in flight. If its balance in flight is disturbed, it must be able to regain it.

Although there are many aspects influencing the stability of a plane, the following are the most important for a paper plane :

- dihedral angle of the wing,
- angle between the wing and horizontal tail plane,
- centre of gravity (CG) of the plane, and
- areas of the tail surfaces.

a) Dihedral angle

The dihedral angle is the angle between the horizontal and the left or the right wing as shown in paragraph 3.9.

A conventional plane with dihedral is more stable in roll than one without dihedral. The dihedral angle is larger for low wing than for high wing planes. It is usually between 10 degrees for high wing and 20 degrees for low wing paper planes.

b) Horizontal tail angle

The tail plane and the wing of an aircraft does not have the same angle relative to the air-flow. The angle is such that the horizontal tail is forced down, ensuring that the wing has a positive angle relative to the flow, which is necessary to produce enough lift. For paper planes the angle between the wing and the horizontal tail can usually be taken as 2.5 degrees.

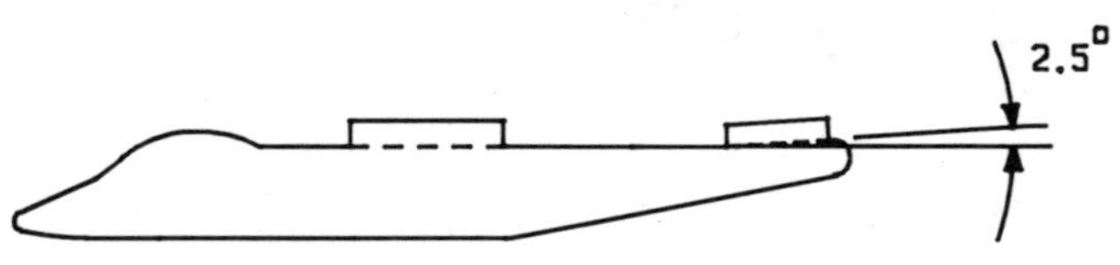

c) Centre of gravity

The best position for the centre of gravity (CG) for the plane depends on the position of the centre or centroid of the wing area (CA). This centre for a non-rectangular wing can be established from the figure given below, where the root chord (C_r) and the tip chord (C_t) is decided upon during the preliminary design. With these two known, construct line (1) as shown in the figure. Line (2) is constructed by joining the centres of C_r and C_t on the wing. CA lies at the intersection of lines (1) and (2). Construct a horizontal line (3) through this intersection to locate the CG. (A vertical line through this intersection gives the mean aerodynamic chord (MAC) which is the aerodynamic representative chord of the wing.)

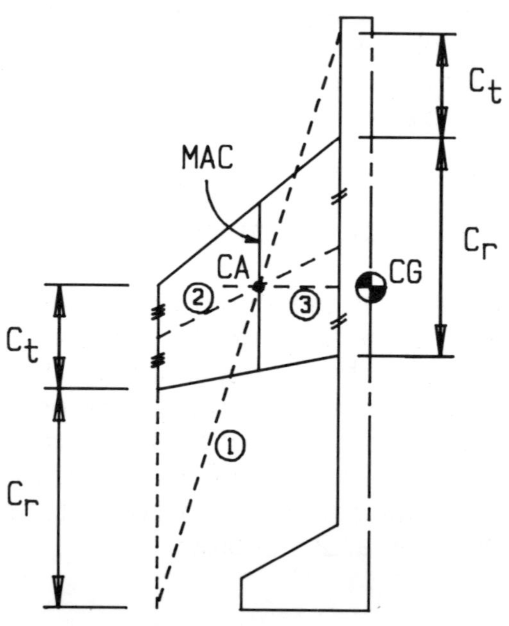

d) Tail areas

The vertical and horizontal tail surfaces control the airplane in flight to provide satisfactory stability characteristics in pitch (nose up or down) and yaw (nose left or right). The calculation of the required tail areas is complex. They are usually not reliable and must be checked by wind tunnel tests, which also have not proven reliable because of scale effects. However, during preliminary design the following formulae are used which are also applicable to paper planes :

$$S_{HT} = (C_{HT}\ S_W\ MAC) / L_{HT} \qquad (2)$$

$$S_{VT} = (C_{VT}\ S_W\ b) / L_{VT} \qquad (3)$$

where

- S_{HT} = the horizontal tail area
- S_{VT} = the vertical tail area
- S_W = the wing area
- MAC = mean aerodynamic chord of wing
- b = wing span
- L_{HT} = distance from CA of the horizontal tail to the CA of the wing
- L_{VT} = distance from CA of the vertical tail to the CA of the wing
- C_{HT} = horizontal tail volume coefficient
- C_{VT} = vertical tail volume coefficient

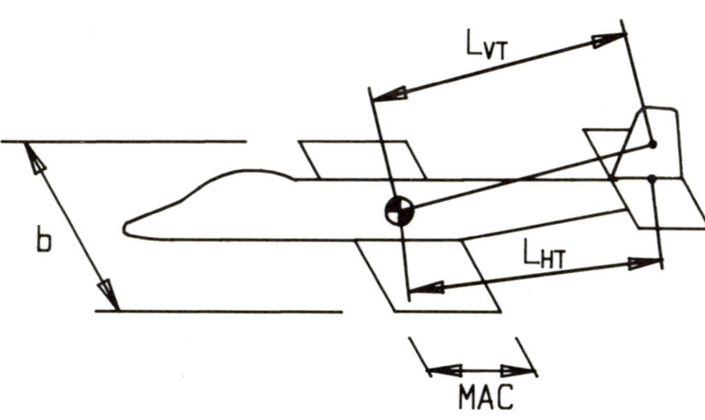

If the preliminary design of the wing planform and the positions of the tail surfaces on the fuselage have been finalised the tail areas can now easily be established if the tail volume coefficients are known. As a guide we can examine these coefficients for well-known full-scale aircraft.

Aircraft	C_{HT}	C_{VT}
Boeing 737-200	1.20	0.097
Boeing 747	1.10	0.084
Douglas DC-9-15	1.20	0.065
Douglas DC-10-10	0.75	0.066

Corning (see reference in Chapter 7) suggests that values of 1.10 and 0.08 for C_{HT} and C_{VT} respectively can be used for jet transport aircraft. The value of 1.10 for C_{HT} is acceptable for paper planes.However, paper planes need smaller vertical fins than full-scale aircraft, which means that C_{VT} must be smaller than 0.08. It is advisable to use a value of 0.06 for C_{VT}. Large vertical fins tend to induce spirals during flight.

It is suggested that you start off with a vertical fin area calculated by means of a C_{VT} value of 0.06. Test fly the paper plane and then gradually decrease the vertical area until the plane tends to "wiggle its tail". This instability is called a "Dutch Roll". Now use a vertical fin area a bit larger than the one that produced the "wiggle".

Note that full-scale aircraft are usually spiral unstable with little "Dutch Roll" tendencies. If you want to scale down the full-scale design, remember that the full-scale vertical fin should not be scaled directly but calculated by means of equation (3). The final vertical fin area should then be established by means of the above-mentioned trial-and-error test flight procedure.

With your experience acquired up to now and with a little bit of practice, you should be able to design your own paper planes.

7. PAPER HELICOPTER DESIGN

Similar to paper plane design the important aspects to consider when designing paper helicopters are flight performance, stability and structural strength. The flight performance of a paper helicopter is not as spectacular as that of a paper plane, due to the many constraints on paper helicopter design. The biggest problem with helicopters, and therefore also paper helicopters, is stability. This aspect for paper helicopters will thus be treated in more detail in this Chapter.

7.1 STABILITY

The ring of the paper helicopter is basically a flying wing. A section through the ring is shown schematically in the next figure. The lift force (L) on the front and rear wing portions can be approximated by the following equation :

$$L = 3.8\,A\,V^2\,\theta \qquad (4)$$

where L = Lift force
A = Wing area
V = Air speed of helicopter
θ = Angle of attack of wing section

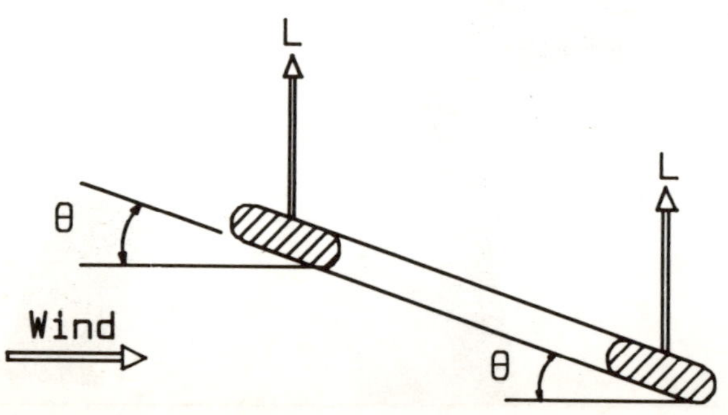

If the front and the rear lift forces are equal, the helicopter will fly forward in a straight line. However, if the ring is bent upwards, as shown in the next figure, the two lift forces will not be equal anymore. The angle of attack of the front wing section (θ_1) will be larger than that of the rear section (θ_2). From equation (4) it can now be seen that the lift force (L_1) on the front wing section will be greater than the force (L_2) on the rear wing due to the different angles of attack.

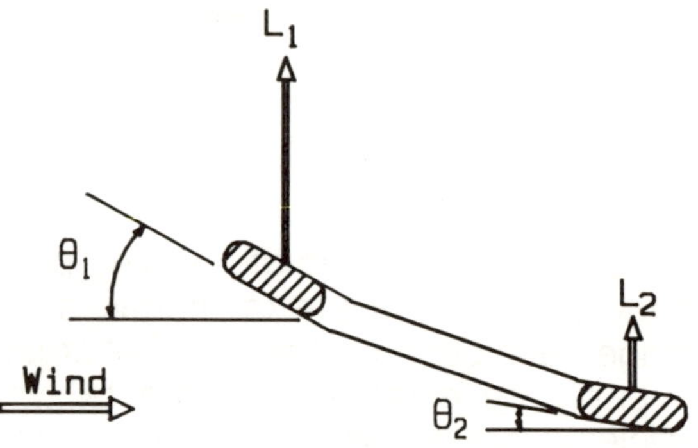

When the ring is rotated the force system is also rotated by 90° in the direction of rotation as a result of the gyroscope effect. This means that the lift forces will now act on the sides of the ring although they were initially generated by the front and the rear portions of the helicopter ring. As these forces are not equal they cause a moment around axis X-X shown in the next figure. Consequently the helicopter will turn to the left during flight.

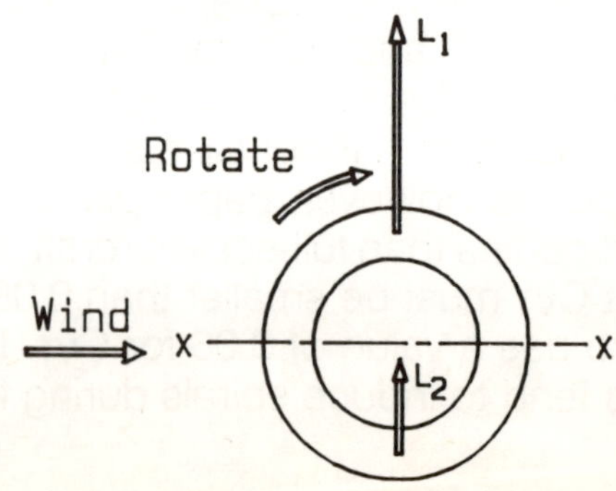

Stability can be achieved by using the trim tabs as shown in the figure below. These tabs act as extensions to the wing sections. When they are bent upwards the effective angle of attack (θ) of the front wing section will become smaller while that of the rear will become larger. By carefully adjusting the trim tabs, the front and rear portions will now look similar, resulting in equal front and rear lift forces. The helicopter will again be stable in flight.

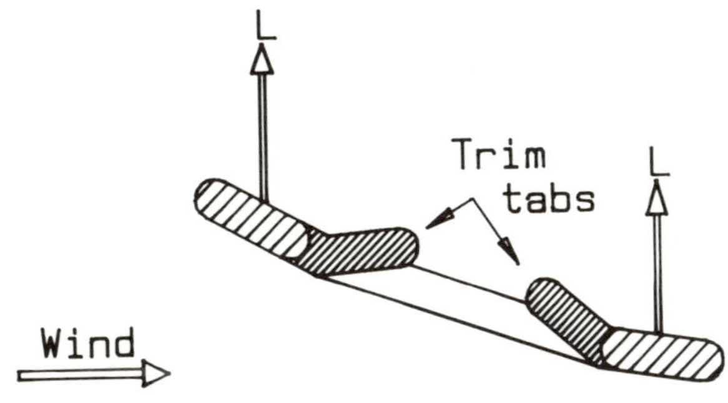

7.2 OTHER ASPECTS

When designing the helicopter ring, keep in mind that the diameter should be as large as possible with a fairly small wing section. However, the ring must have enough strength and stiffness.

Any design can be chosen for the helicopter fuselage. The rear fin of the fuselage must be fairly large to ensure that the fuselage always points in the flight direction. Structural strength of the fuselage can be achieved by various layers of paper, where the direction of stiffness of the paper coincides with the lengthwise direction of the fuselage.

The paper helicopter will be more stable in flight if the centre of gravity of the fuselage is directly below the rotation axis of the ring.

8. REFERENCES

Paper Flight, J. Botermans, Holt, Rinehart & Winston, New York.

Supersonic and subsonic CTOL and VTOL airplane design, G. Corning, University of Maryland, Maryland.

Observer's Book of Aircraft, W. Green, Frederick Warne, London.

Paper Airplanes, M. Arceneaux, Troubadour Press, Inc., San Francisco.

The Paper Airplane Book, A.L. Hammond and A. Fujino (eds), Vintage Books, New York.

White Wings, Y. Ninomiya, AG Industries Inc., Redmond.

The Best Paper Aircraft, C. Morris, The Putnam Publishing Group, New York.

Fantastic Paper Planes, M. Johnson, Penguin Books, London.

The Great International Paper Airplane Book, J. Mander, G. Dippel and H. Gossage, Simon and Schuster, New York.

The Ultimate Paper Airplane, R. Kline, Simon and Schuster, New York.

30 Planes for the Paper Pilot, P. Vollheim, Wallaby Books, Pocket Books, New York.

Flying Dinosaurs, M. Johnson, Penguin, London.

SIAI Marchetti S.211

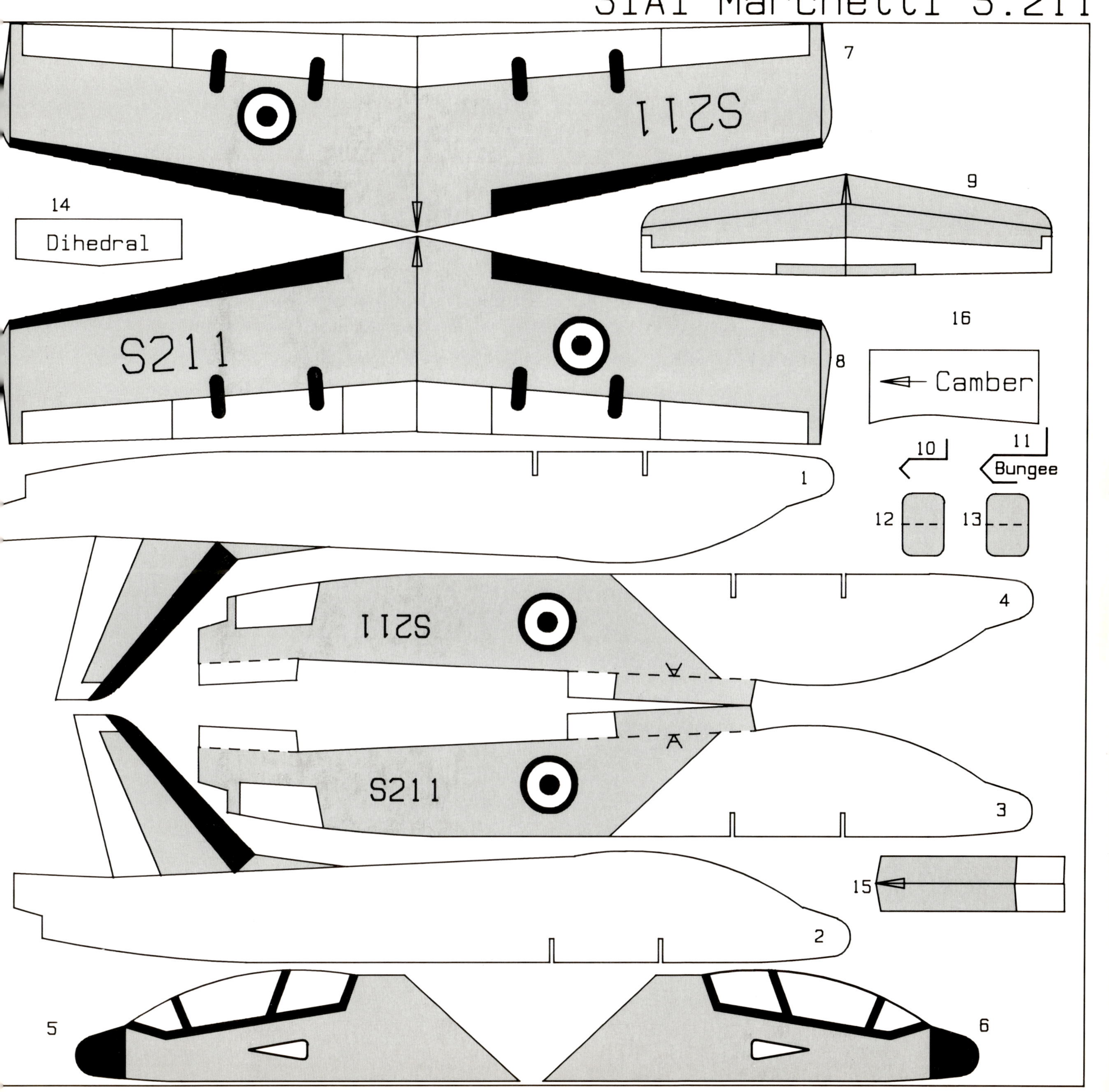

GRUMMAN HAWKEYE

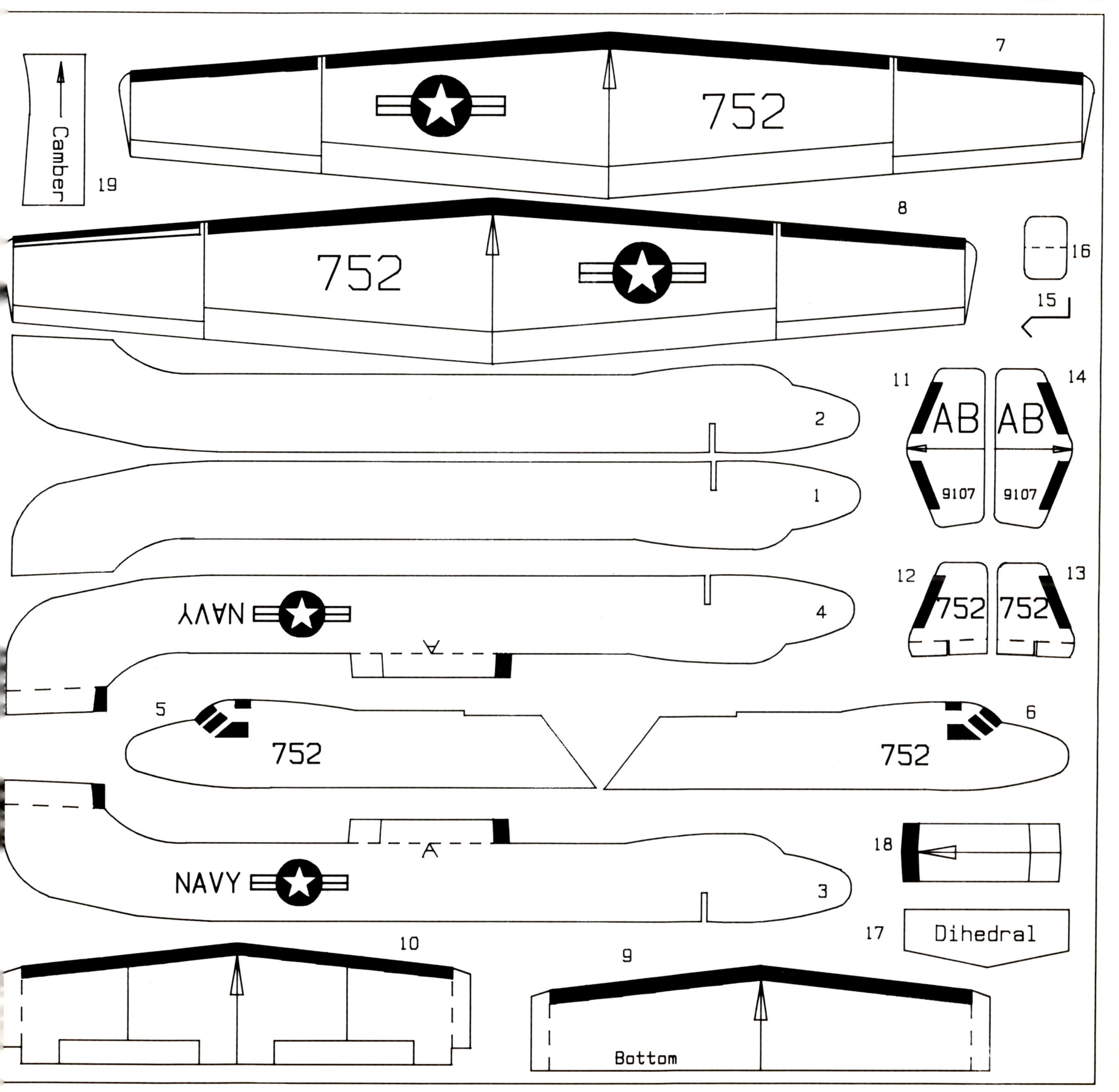

ROCKWELL B-1B

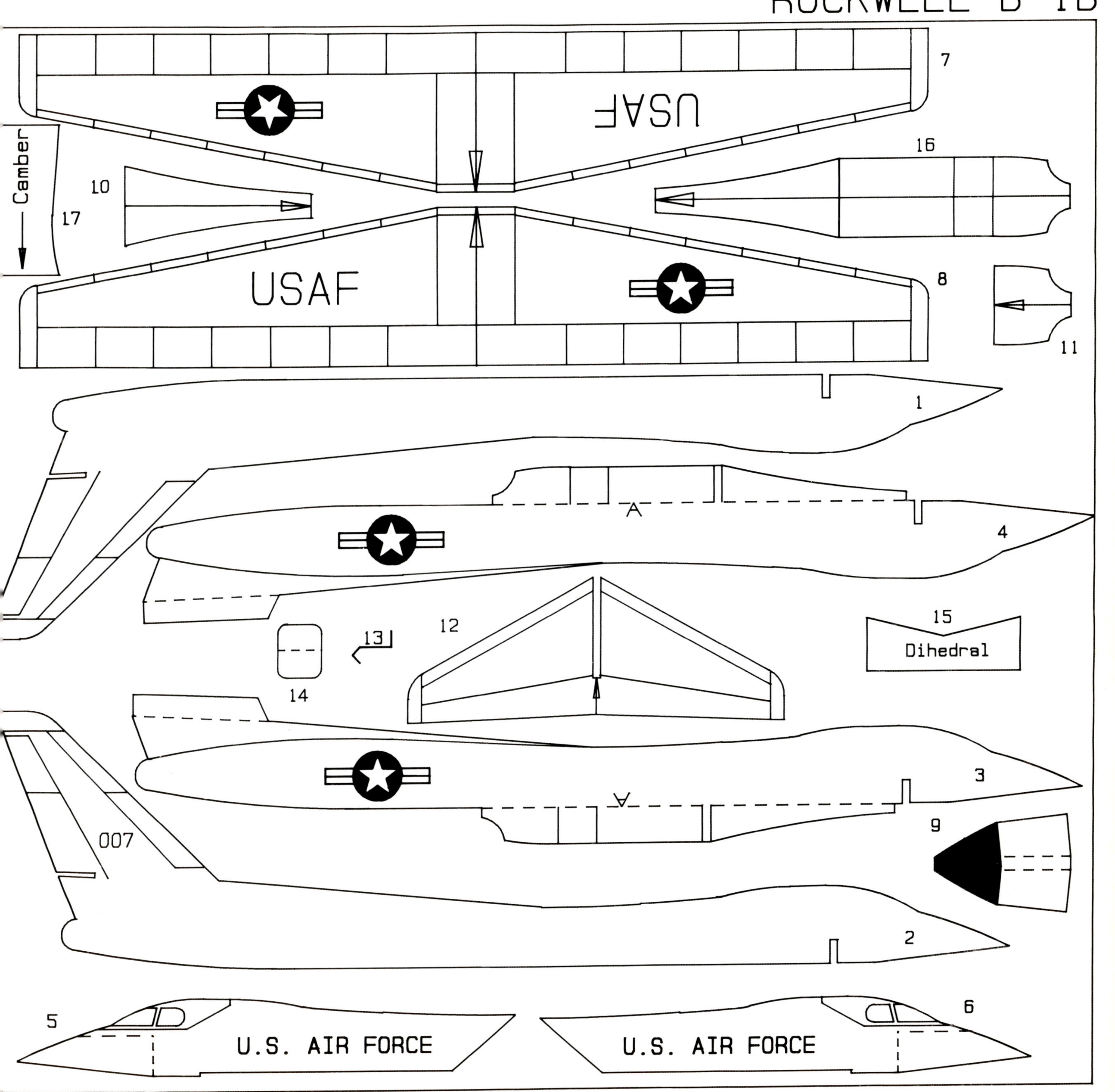

CESSNA Caravan

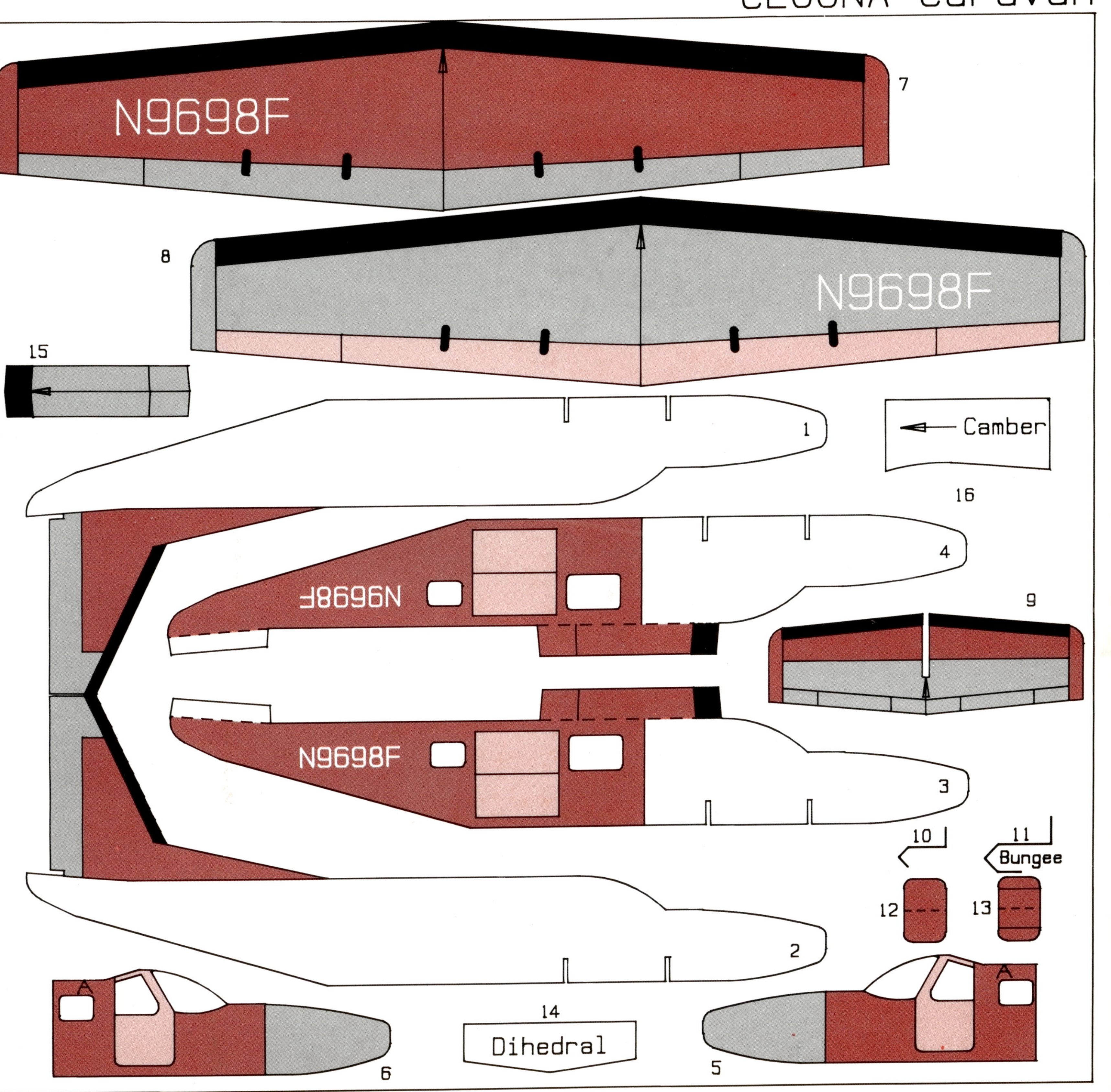

Bizjet

7
N560CC
15
Dihedral
17
Camber
8
N560CC
10 Right Engine
Rolls Royce
14
13
1
N560CC
N560CC
4
11
5
6
12
N560CC
N560CC
3
16
2
Rolls Royce
9 Left Engine

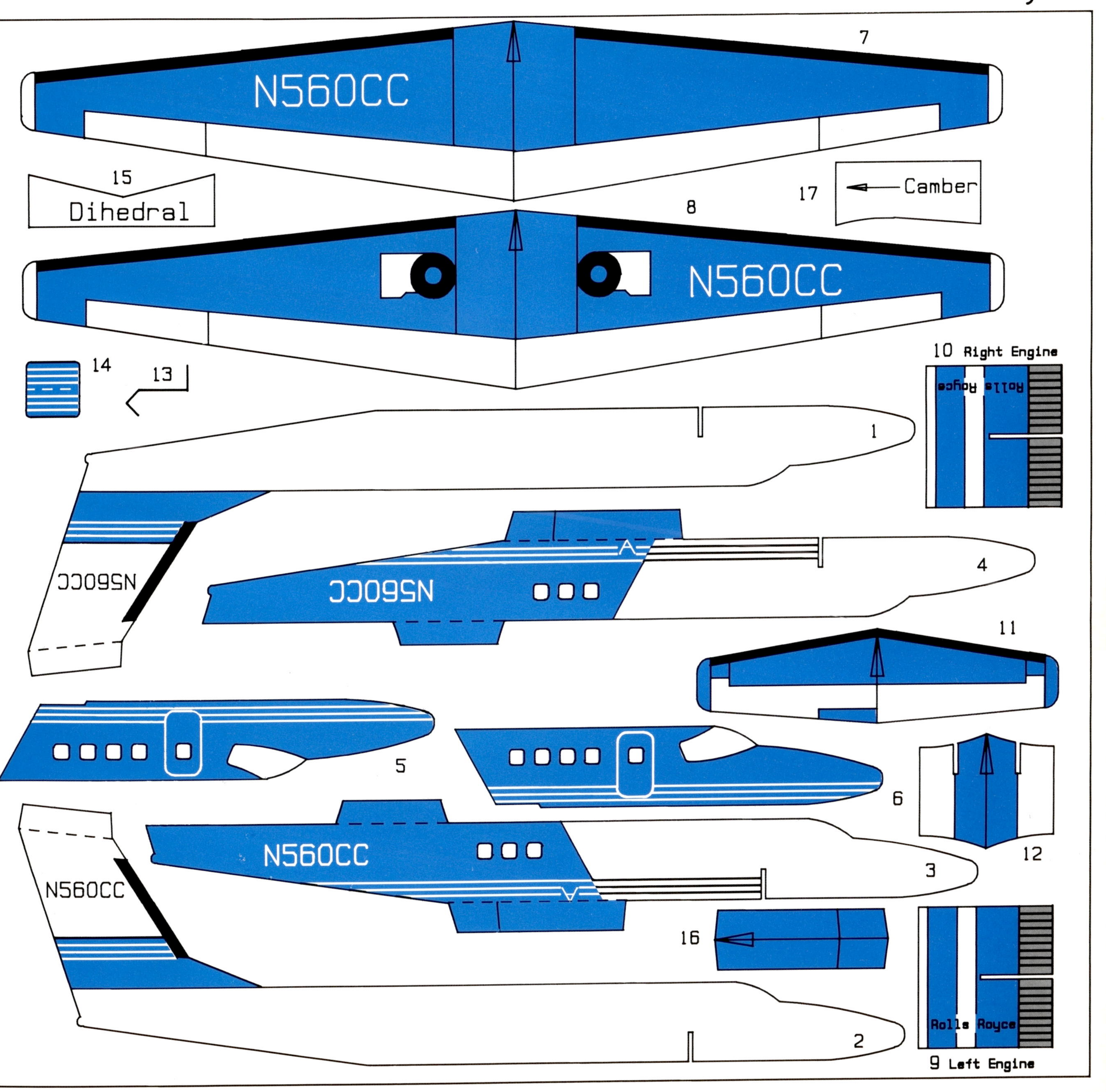

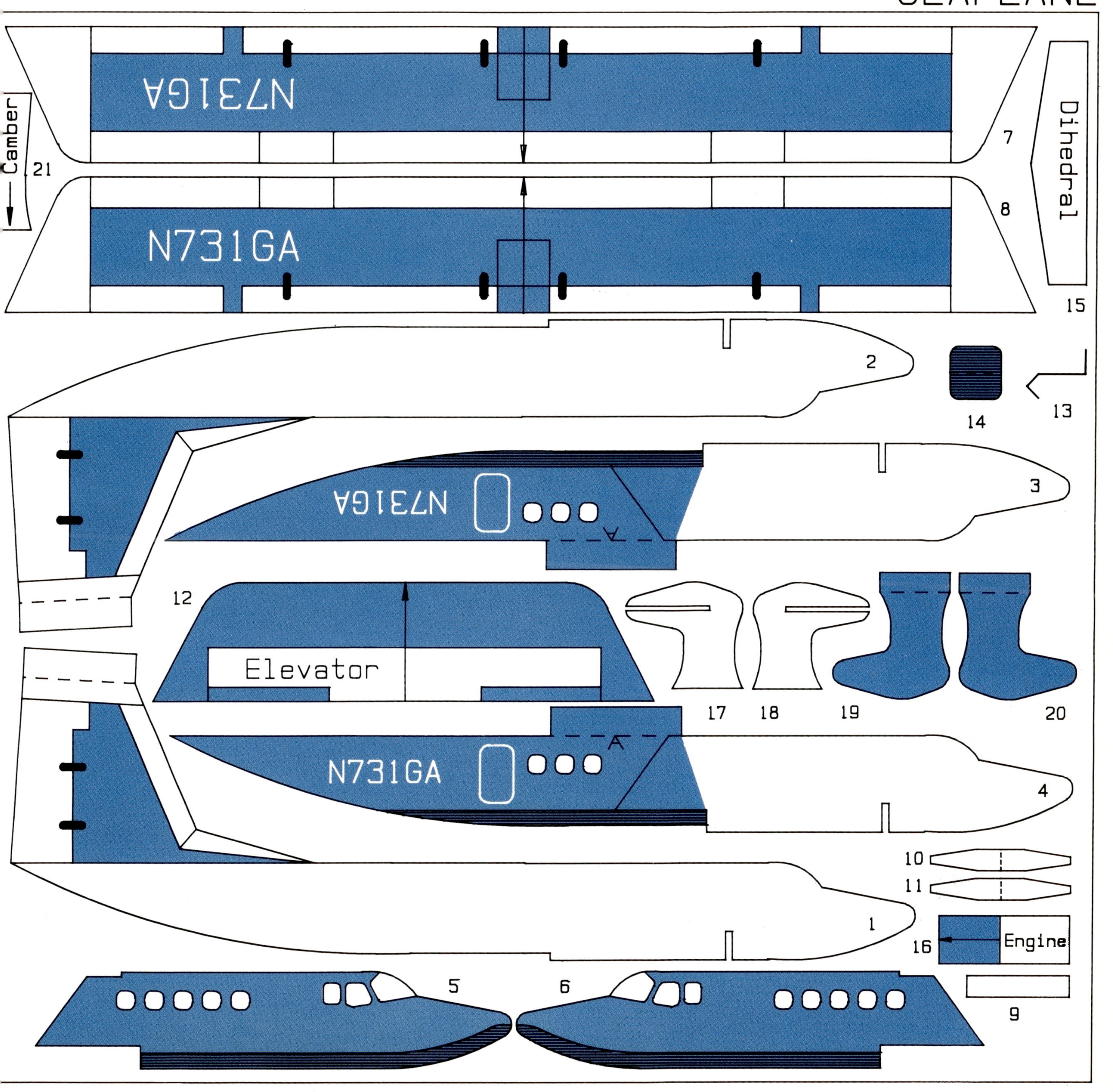
Camber
21
N731GA
N731GA
7
8
Dihedral
15
2
14
13
N731GA
3
A
12
Elevator
17
18
19
20
A
N731GA
4
10
11
1
16
Engine
5
6
9

FAMA IA 63 PAMPA

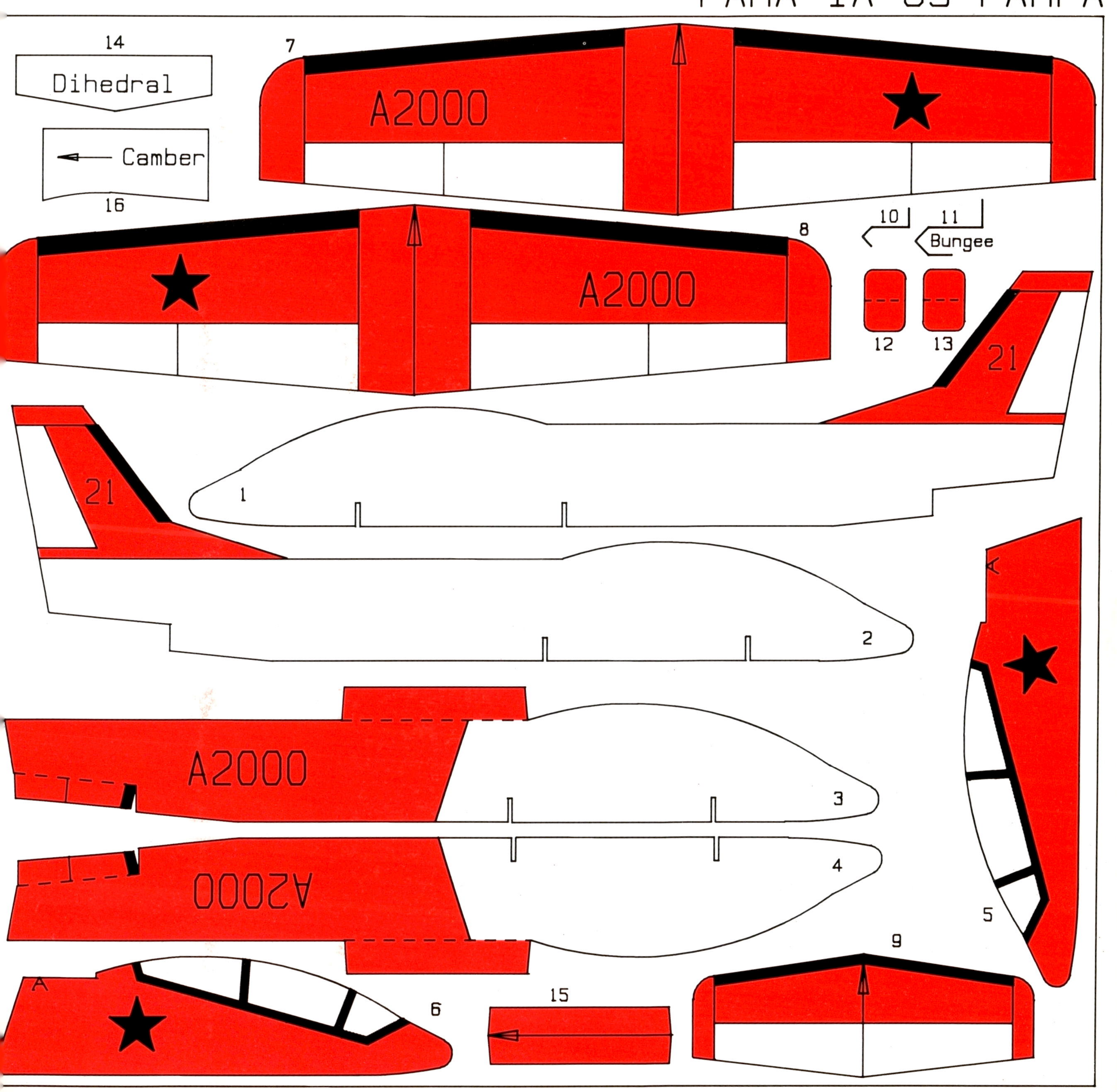

SPACE SHUTTLE

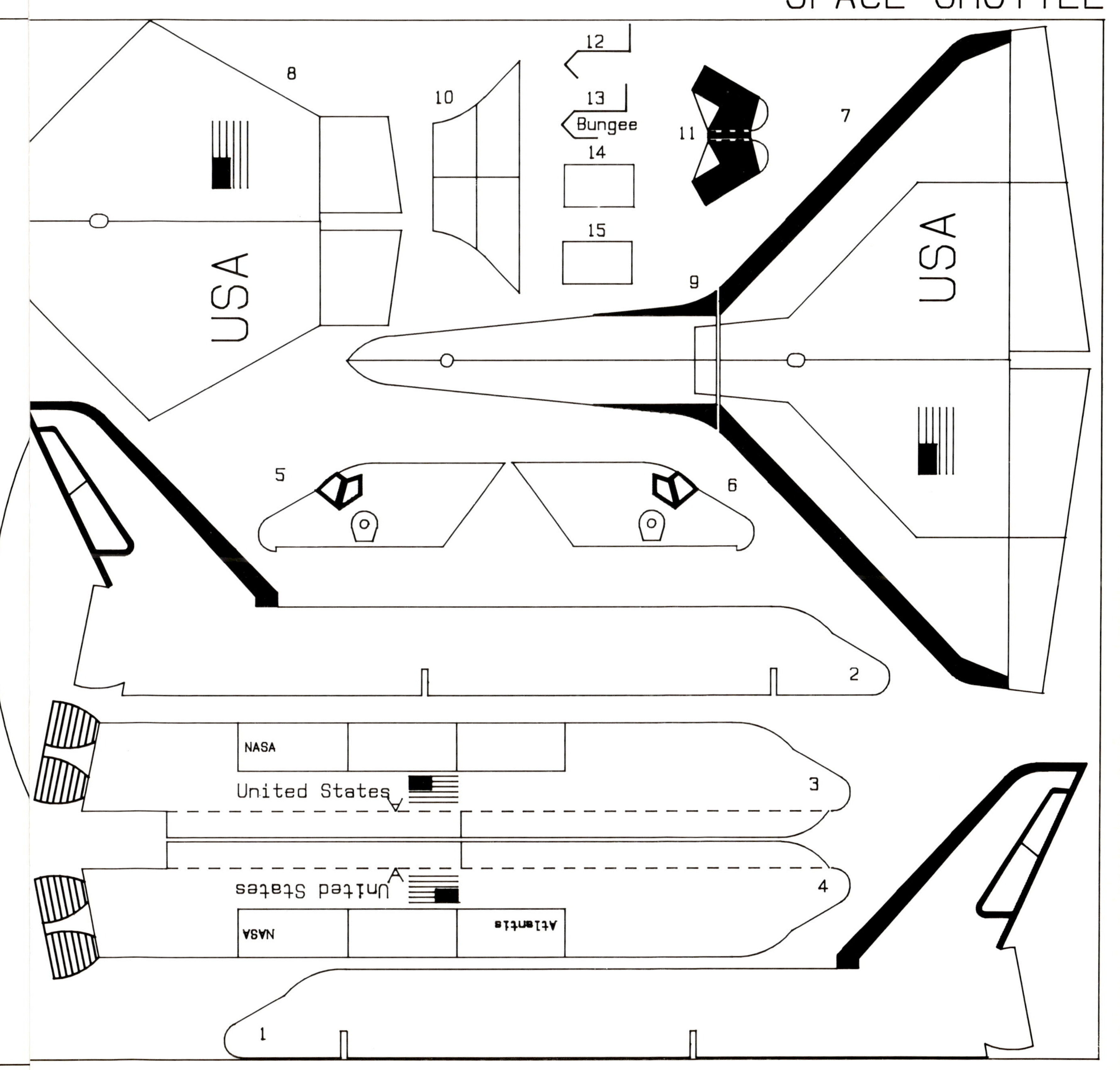

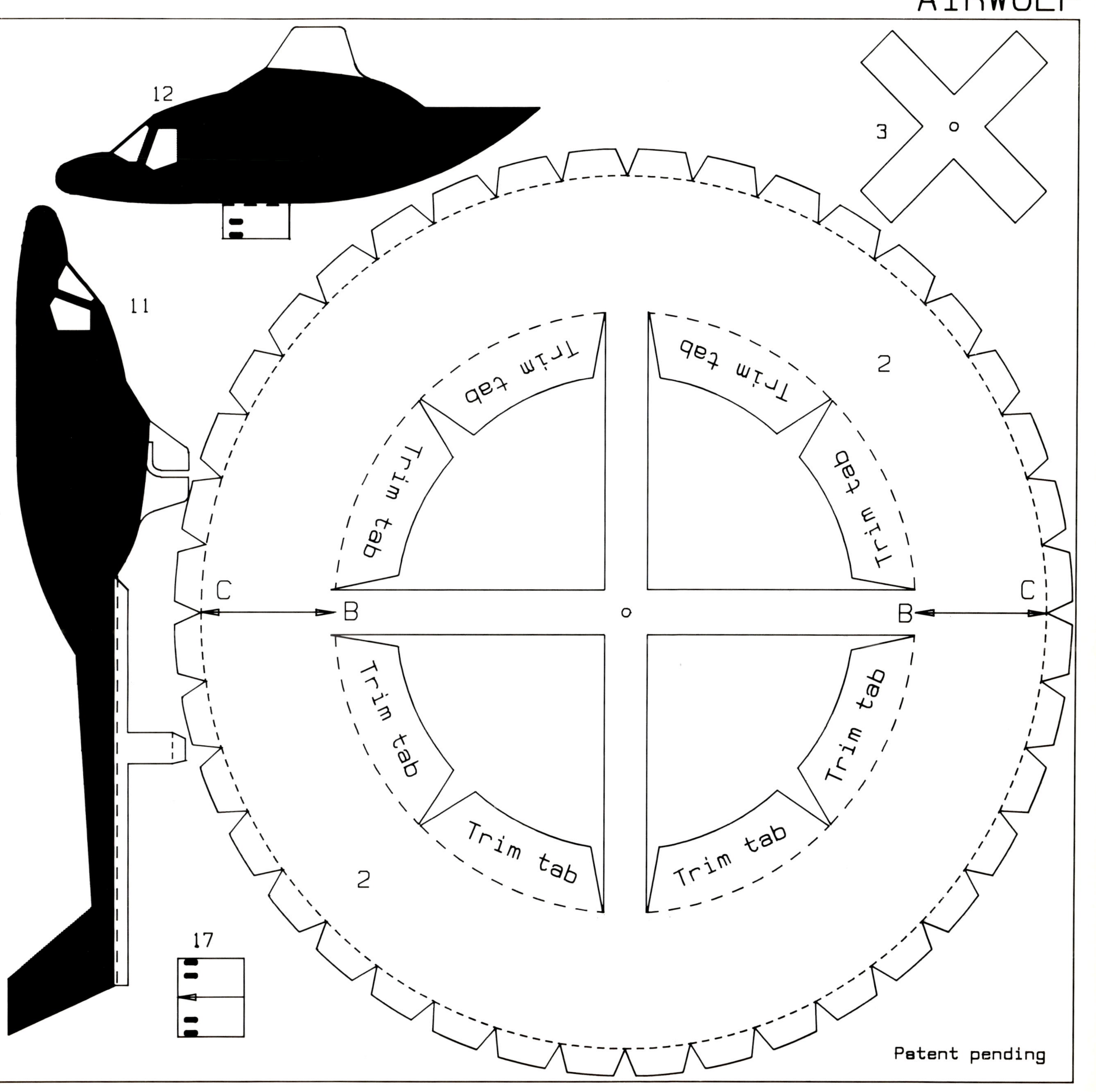
12
3
11
2
Trim tab
Trim tab
Trim tab
Trim tab
C
B
B
C
Trim tab
Trim tab
Trim tab
Trim tab
2
17
Patent pending